Proof Positive

Proof Positive

by Peter Lerangis

AN
APPLE
PAPERBACK

SCHOLASTIC INC.
New York Toronto London Auckland Sydney
Mexico City New Delhi Hong Kong Buenos Aires

12 11 10 9 8 7 6 5 4 3 2 1   5 6 7 8 9 10/0
                                                 40
Printed in the U.S.A.
First printing, January 2005

Chapter One

"Mom!" shouted Andrew Wall. "*Mo-o-o-o-om!*"

Too late. He hadn't made the green light. His voice was swallowed up by the whoosh of traffic on Beach Street. A few startled tourists shook their heads in sympathy, thinking he was another lost kid in the Big City.

But Andrew wasn't lost. He knew exactly where he was — stuck on a corner of Fisherman's Wharf, a few blocks from his house in San Francisco. He knew where he *wanted* to be, too — across the street, on a cable car that was now climbing uphill toward the center of the city. If he'd been just a little faster — if his twin sister, Evie, hadn't pulled him back — he'd be there now. He'd be with Mom.

Squinting into the bright California sunshine, Andrew tried to pick her out among the passengers, but the car was too crowded and too far away.

"Are you sure it was her?" Evie asked.

"*I know what Mom looks like!*" Andrew snapped. "Why did you stop me, Evie?"

Evie shrugged. "Are you crazy? You would have been roadkill."

"The light was yellow! I would have been on the other side by now!"

"Right. With the help of your Intergalactic Stop-Time Sneakers and Ray-Gun?"

Andrew held back the urge to throttle her. Evie was *always* doing this, acting like she was smarter — just because she was four minutes older! Always accusing him of living in a fantasy. Okay, maybe it was true. Sometimes life got boring. Sometimes it was better to be a Bombardier or a space warrior instead of an average almost-twelve-year-old kid named Andrew Wall. But so what? It didn't mean he was *always* in a dream world. Especially when it came to something serious. Like the disappearance of Cassandra Kane Wall, otherwise known as Mom.

She'd been missing since "11 11 11" — the eleventh day of the eleventh month, on Andrew and Evie's eleventh birthday. No warning, no good-bye — just a hurried note. It hadn't fazed them at first. This kind of thing had happened before. Both Mom and Pop worked for covert government organizations, so the family was used to sudden moves and disappearances. But not like this. As weeks turned into months, Andrew and Evie began to fear the worst.

It wasn't until early this month — September — that the packages began arriving.

The first appeared on their doorstep soon after they'd moved to Connecticut. The contents — a packet of seeds, a key, a kaleidoscope, an odd essay — were clues. When a crabby old next-door neighbor named Mrs. Digitalis turned out to be "Foxglove," a code-breaking ex-colleague of Mom's, the twins began to unlock the truth: Mom was a spy. She had worked for a secret international organization called The Company. She'd found out things she wasn't supposed to know. She was in hiding. In deep trouble. She couldn't count on her friends to find her, because they were all being watched. Her only hope was to make spies out of the people *no one* would suspect — Andrew and Evie.

But when Foxglove was attacked and had to flee, the training suddenly ended. That same night, Pop got emergency transfer orders — to San Francisco. The Walls left the next morning without any notice, not even a phone call to the school administration. No way on earth would Mom be able to track Andrew and Evie.

Or so they thought — until package number two appeared in Andrew's locker at their new school. This package contained a backward-playing cassette tape, an orange sneaker, and some odd messages. More clues, it turned out, were hidden throughout the city — and tricky to find. Especially after Pop hired a nanny, Marisol, to keep track of them.

Letting Marisol help them had been the biggest mistake of Andrew and Evie's lives.

Marisol, it turned out, was a spy. She was working for The Company, to try to find Mom. If it hadn't been for some quick thinking — and an intervention by the Franklins, middle-aged hippie biker friends of Mom — Marisol might have intercepted Mom's messages to Andrew and Evie. And delivered Mom to the enemy.

Now Mr. Franklin was off seeking Mom with the help of a high-tech tracking device called Onyx. And Andrew and Evie had emerged from the adventure shaken, but much wiser. They knew they could count on only two truths:

Nothing was as it seemed. And no one was to be trusted.

Ever.

Seeing Mom — in person, in public — was the last thing they expected.

Blink.

The light turned green, and Andrew sprang.

He flew across Beach Street. Behind him, Evie was

shouting, telling him to stop. But sometimes Evie had to be ignored.

The hill was steep. You needed Schwarzenegger thighs to live in San Francisco. Within half a block, Andrew was panting. Normally he loved the hills and the amazing views, but at the moment, he wished he were someplace flat, like Nebraska.

A hum rose up from inside a narrow metal-edged slot in the center of the street — the transportation cable, which turned underground twenty-four/seven like a hidden escalator. The cable cars moved by means of a lever that reached down into the slot, latching onto the cable for the ride; they stopped by easing off. Mom's car was now three blocks ahead, moving, cresting the hill, full of passengers and about to disappear from sight.

Andrew dug in hard, feeling the burn in his thighs, his lungs. He was panting for air now, *gulping* for air. Flagging. Fast.

BEEP-BEEEEEP!

"Hey, slowpoke! Get in!"

Andrew wheeled around. His sister was yelling at him from the open rear window of a taxi. As the car pulled up to the curb, she flung open the back door. "Don't mean to hurt your feelings, Road Runner," she said, "but this'll be faster."

Andrew wobbled to the curb and slid in silently next to Evie.

"You're welcome," she said.

"Smart aleck," Andrew mumbled.

Evie grinned. "Nope. Just smart."

The driver gunned the accelerator and the engine groaned, working its way up the hill. At the peak, they stopped at a red light. Andrew and Evie could see all the way down Powell to Market Street. The cable car was rolling briskly past Union Square, through bumper-to-bumper traffic on either side of the tracks.

"Can you handle downhill on foot?" Evie asked.

Andrew was out the door before Evie could pay the driver.

She caught up with him at the northwestern corner of Union Square Park. The cable car was two blocks ahead. It had pulled over for its last stop, near Market Street. A line of people, held back by a metal gate, waited to get on while the passengers filed off.

Andrew pointed into the crowd. "There!"

"Where? The one carrying the baby?"

"*No!* The one eating the candy bar!"

"A Skor bar? Mom loves Skor bars."

"*What's the difference?* She's at the end of the block. Look at her hair!"

It was the back of Mom's head — her reddish-brown hair. Familiar as his own image in the mirror. Evie had to believe him now. Mom appeared and disappeared in the throng, walking briskly away from them — then turned into a nondescript brick building.

Andrew sidestepped through the crowd, reaching the front door in seconds. Inside was a small, drab-looking lobby, where an elevator slid shut. Next to the elevator was a set of worn marble stairs.

Andrew pushed his way into the lobby, staring at the line of numbers above the elevator door.

"Let's take the stairs!" Evie said.

"Wait. We'll see where the elevator stops." Andrew watched the floor numbers as they glowed in sequence — L . . . 2 . . . 3 . . . 4. "Straight to the top floor. She must be getting off there."

Evie scampered ahead, taking the stairs two at a time, but Andrew lagged behind. His thighs, still recovering from the hill, were screaming.

Soon Evie was calling down from the top. "She's not here. Now what?"

Andrew dragged himself to the fourth-floor landing. There was only one door here, a thick industrial metal slab decorated with a faded gold logo:

Mission Accomplished.

"Aha — an obvious . . . front . . ." Andrew said, catching his breath, "for a secret . . . government task force . . ."

From inside came a low, rhythmic pounding. Evie gave her brother a dubious look. "Spy music?" she said, reaching for the latch.

"Be prepared," Andrew said. "This may require special access — like the right fingerprints, or the pattern in your eye, or a digital voice profile . . ."

Evie pulled the door open.

No alarm. No flashing lights.

Just the surging beat of an old freestyle dance tune.

"Looks like an exercise class," Evie said.

A polished wood floor stretched out into a room lined with mirrors. On one side of the room, a trim woman in tights was stretching, supporting herself on a long wooden ballet barre. On the other side, a few dozen other people were crouching over gym bags.

Andrew glanced around, scrutinizing each face. "Physical training," he explained. "A spy needs to be ready, mentally and —"

There.

She was squatting in the back, turned away from them, pulling her hair back.

"Sighted," Andrew whispered, his voice choking with emotion. "The one with the scrunchy."

Evie narrowed her eyes. "Mom hates scrunchies."

Andrew stepped inside and began to run, not even aware of his aching thighs. The chase was over. She was here — after *ten months!* He fought back tears of joy. His footsteps thumped loudly against the floor as his shout — "*MO-O-O-M!*" — echoed off the mirrored walls.

The instructor jumped. At once, all conversation in the room stopped.

Every woman spun around to look at him.

And Andrew stopped in his tracks.

Mom was looking at him, too.

But her face was totally wrong — bony, not softly rounded. Brown eyes, not green.

"Um," Andrew said uncertainly. "Plastic surgery?"

"I beg your pardon?" the woman replied, in a low-pitched voice Andrew had never heard before.

Evie grabbed his shoulder from behind. "Uh, please excuse my brother. He walks in his sleep. Babbles. Total nonsense. Guess he didn't take his meds today."

"I — I thought . . ." Andrew stammered.

In the glare of two dozen pairs of eyes, Evie yanked her brother toward the door. "You, Andrew Wall, are in huge trouble."

Chapter Two

STEP-STEP-falap-falap-falap-STEP-STEP-falap-falap-falap . . .

Andrew slammed his door. Even up here on the third floor, he could hear Evie's tap-dancing in the basement.

Tap-dancing relieved stress, according to Evie. *Stress YOU caused*, she'd said, *with your dumb fantasy that you saw Mom.*

Okay, okay, so he'd been wrong. It was embarrassing to mistake someone else for your mom. He'd suffered, too, but he didn't punish the whole house for it. Why couldn't Evie pick a normal, *quiet* way to relieve stress — like reading?

Andrew stood at his window, letting the ocean breeze play across his face. In the setting sun, the red-orange cables of the Golden Gate Bridge looked as if they'd caught fire. A section of Alcatraz Island poked between the peaks of the houses like a giant turtle stuck in its journey across the bay.

He wished with all his heart that his mom were here

right now. She used to say *A fantasy life is like a kite. Hold on to it as long as you can, and let it soar.* He didn't believe that anymore. Not after today. Seeing Mom in a stranger's face was worse than a fantasy. It felt scary. Like he was losing control. What was the point of holding on to a kite if it pulled you off the ground?

From downstairs he could hear Pop talking on the phone, chuckling, tossing numbers around, making things work out. Richard Henry Wall, World's Greatest Problem Solver. Nothing fazed Pop. You could tell him a pink-striped rhino was reciting poetry on the front lawn — and he'd calmly tell you about the green one he saw in Upper Volta. *He'd* know just what to say about this afternoon. But asking for Pop's help was out of the question. It would mean explaining *why* Andrew thought he'd seen Mom in San Francisco. Which would mean explaining the boxes. The codes. The equipment. Foxglove. And the true identity of the "nanny" Pop had hired.

Mom's instructions had been clear: Pop wasn't to know about *anything*. Which made sense. Mom's enemies would have their eyes on Pop. They'd be *waiting* for Mom to contact him. She had to keep him out of it. To protect him.

Of course, now that Andrew and Evie had blabbed to Marisol, The Company would be watching them, too.

And that meant it was no longer safe for Mom to send them boxes or clues or spy equipment. Mom's last chance was Mr. Franklin and the Onyx tracking device. Wherever *they* were.

Andrew slumped on the bed. Confiding in Marisol had been stupid, stupid, *stupid*. He and Evie had failed their own mother.

The sudden bleep of his cell phone made him jump. That was another thing. Pop had given the phone to Andrew and Evie to share — to keep track of them until he could find another nanny. He was still sore at them about Marisol. He thought they'd "been mean" to her and "scared her away."

"Hello?" Andrew said, snatching up the receiver.

"I'll have one large pepperoni and a medium half-mushroom, half-extra-cheese, for pickup," a voice said.

Andrew sighed. It was the third call he'd gotten like this. Their cell number must have belonged to a pizza place that went out of business. "Sorry, wrong number," he said.

STEP-STEP-FALAP-FALAP-FALAP-STEP-STEP-FALAP-FALAP-FALAP . . .

Evie's taps were growing stronger by the minute.

Andrew turned off the phone, put a thick pillow over his ears, and closed his eyes.

When he opened them again, the taps had stopped. The room was dark except for his night-light, which illuminated a glass of water and a metal tray on his night table. He lifted the cover and was greeted by a plate of congealed spaghetti, a few withered string beans, and a note from Pop:

Bon appetit, Rip Van Winkle! There's some cold Gatorade in the fridge.

That was one talent Pop definitely lacked. Making dinner.

Andrew glanced at his desk clock — 3:07 A.M. — and turned over, groaning at the pain in his thighs, which had gotten worse . . .

Thump.

A noise. From the garage.

Weird. Pop often went to work at odd hours, but he always made a loud announcement first.

Maybe Andrew had slept through it.

He sat up and gingerly shifted his aching legs around. Sliding his feet into slippers, he tiptoed into the hallway. As he made his way down the carpeted stairway, he heard Evie murmuring in her sleep. On the second floor, a steady snore buzzed from Pop's bedroom.

A squirrel? A raccoon? It was probably no big deal. Still, it was worth checking the garage. Better to be safe. A spy was always cautious.

Andrew Wall, Private Eye, slips down to the first floor of the Secret Lair, his footsteps as quiet as the lonely flutter of a moth wing. He turned on all the lights as he walked through the foyer, the living room, the kitchen . . . and then down the stairs into the basement.

On the far wall he spies the door to the underground laboratory, hidden from nefarious villains by elaborate security and shape-shifting techniques. The garage door was closed. It and the light switch were on the far wall, next to a rack full of keys. Andrew flicked on the switch and turned the knob. The door had been left unlocked.

Note to self: Never again leave security in the hands of Trudy Turbo-Toes, the Tap-dancing Terror. He looked into the garage. Pop's car was nestled snugly into the small space, surrounded by a thousand shadows — hoses, tools, cans, bicycles, sports equipment. He could see Pop's favorite gadget, a Global Positioning System, Velcroed to the dashboard. "Hello?" he called out cautiously.

No answer. Good.

He pulled the door shut and locked it. As he turned to go back upstairs, he caught a glimpse of the key rack, with its carefully labeled hooks — Gym locker . . . Spare house keys . . . Andrew . . . Evie . . . Pop . . .

Pop's hook, he noticed, was empty. Which was strange, considering Pop had trained Andrew and Evie *always* to put their keys on the hooks. Pop was a military man — procedure all the way. Andrew grinned. Mr. Perfect was losing his edge.

Evildoers thwarted again, Private Eye Wall shuts off the lights and heads back upstairs for a well-deserved night of sleep . . .

"*Kids . . . ?* Have either of you seen my car keys?"

Pop's voice woke Andrew way too early the next morning. He was standing in Andrew's door, the band of grayish-brown hair that circled his balding head brushed into submission, his charcoal-gray suit buttoned just so. He gave off a faint scent of the bay rum cologne Andrew bought him every Christmas.

"Ahem." Andrew summoned up his best Pop-voice imitation: "Returning your keys to the rack is a useful habit. And useful habits are signs of an organized mind!"

"Okay, okay. Looks like I'm taking the bus today." Pop smiled sheepishly. "You two come right home after school, you hear?"

"Waffle cones with three scoops if we find your keys?" Evie called from her bedroom.

Pop muttered a noncommittal answer as he raced down the stairs and out the front door.

Andrew slowly got out of bed, working out the cramp in his thighs. He felt creaky, like Frankenstein's monster. Staggering past his desk, he grabbed his cell phone and turned it on. 1 MISSED CALL, the screen said.

He accessed his voice mail. A medium sausage and peppers. He had to figure out some way to block all those pizza orders.

Erasing the message, Andrew tapped his computer mouse. His screen came to life, and he squinted at his e-mails. The usual spams and sci-fi/fantasy Web group messages.

Evie strolled into his room. "Have you gotten ready yet?"

"Have you heard of knocking?" Andrew groused, highlighting all the junk mail that had somehow made it past the filter.

DELETE. DELETE. DELETE. DELETE . . .

At the last message, time-stamped 4:09 A.M., he stopped. "Evie, look at this . . ."

With a heavy sigh, Evie looked over his shoulder.

F	A	E		C	O	K	E
M	I	N	T	Y		O	X	Y
U	N	G	I		B	U	R
I	S		D	R	U	N	K

"It's spam," Evie said.

"Spam tries to sell stuff," Andrew said. "This looks like code."

"'Citizen Berlin'? 'Fae Coke minty oxy ungi bur is drunk'? It's *German* spam. Don't get your hopes up again, Andrew. Have you already forgotten what happened yesterday afternoon?"

He hadn't, of course. Every detail was still painfully replaying inside his head. But this time Evie was wrong. Andrew was sure of it. He recognized code when he saw it. "Think about it, Evie. Maybe Mom can't send us a package — but she *can* send e-mails! Okay . . . there must be a *key* — some clue to help us solve the code. Mom always sends a key. It could be the 'From' line. Or this 'Subject' line. 'Move like a dumbwaiter.' That's it! *Evie, she's talking about that guy at Olive Garden who brought me fried clams when I asked for French fries!* It *has* to be Mom!"

"Not a *dumb waiter*. A *dumbwaiter*, one word. It's a small elevator. It carries food from a kitchen up and down to the other floors of a building. I read about it in an Agatha Christie book."

"Okay, so maybe we're supposed to jump up and down while we read this?"

Evie grudgingly knelt beside him and looked at the message. "I don't think so. The words are placed in a grid. Scrambled. Each letter is in its own box. The boxes are arranged in rows and columns —"

"Aha," Andrew said, sitting on the edge of his bed. "Rows go across — and columns go *up and down*."

"Thank you, Professor Einstein. Now, if this *is* a code — and I'm not saying it is — what if we move the *letters* up or down? Like, shift them around but keep them in the same column?"

Andrew glanced at the first word in the upper left-hand column, and at the letters beneath it:

F	A	E
M	I	N
U	N	G
I	S	

In his mind, he slid the N up and the E down. "So . . . that top word could be FAN . . ." he said, then shifted other letters: ". . . or possibly FIN, MAN, IAN, USE —"

"USE . . . well, if it were a note from Mom, that would make sense. Mom's notes are instructions. 'Use' is the first word of an instruction."

Andrew grabbed a sheet of graph paper from his desk and gave it to his sister. "You do it. My legs hurt."

Evie grabbed the paper. Good. She was coming around. She believed him.

Carefully, she wrote out the letters in the grid, and then rearranged them:

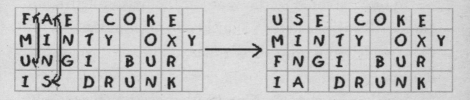

Now Andrew eyed the word on the upper right and the letters under it:

"If you move the N to the top and switch it with the K, you get CONE," Andrew said. "You can also make CONK . . . YOKE . . ."

"Or YOUR!" Evie blurted out. "'USE YOUR'!"

On her graph paper, she shifted around the letters on the right side — exchanging one for the other, erasing, filling, replacing:

U	S	E		C	O	K	E	
M	I	N	T	Y	O	X	Y	
F	N	G	I		B	U	R	
I	A		D	R	U	N	K	

→

U	S	E		Y	O	U	R
M	I	N	T	C		O	X	Y
F	N	G	I		B	K	E
I	A		D	R	U	N	K

Andrew pointed to the word at the bottom left-hand corner. "Okay, the letter S is locked in place at the top. So this two-letter word — IA — has to be IN. No other options."

Evie looked closely. "Same with that BKE. It can only be BOX! Andrew, look, this is starting to make sense!"

U	S	E		Y	O	U	R
M	I	N	T	C		O	X	Y
F	N	G	I		B	K	E
I	A		D	R	U	N	K

→

U	S	E		Y	O	U	R
M	I	N	T	C		K	E	Y
F	A	G	I		B	O	X
I	N		D	R	U	N	K

"Use your . . . *something* . . . key!" Andrew exclaimed. "Is she talking about the key she sent us in Connecticut — the one that opens any lock?"

Evie's eyes widened. "You see those three letters, A, G, I? If we move them up, we get . . ."

U	S	E		Y	O	U	R
M	I	K	N	K	T	K	C		K	E	Y
F	A	G	I		B	O	X
I	N		D	R	U	N	K

→

U	S	E		Y	O	U	R
M	A	G	I	C		K	E	Y
F	I	N	T		B	O	X
I	N		D	R	U	N	K

Andrew looked at Evie. Evie looked at Andrew. "Go for it," he said.

Evie quickly did one last rearrangement:

U	S	E		Y	O	U	R
M	A	G	I	C		K	E	Y
F	I	N	T		B	O	X
I	N		D	R	U	N	K

→

U	S	E		Y	O	U	R
M	A	G	I	C		K	E	Y
F	I	N	D		B	O	X
I	N		T	R	U	N	K

"The trunk of the car . . ." Andrew said. "Evie . . . I heard this bump in the middle of the night, from the garage. I went down there, but the place was empty!"

"Mom was *here?*" Evie shook her head. "Andrew, this bothers me. Mom's not supposed to be giving us boxes anymore. We're suspects. The Company is tailing us. Marisol knows about us."

Andrew's eyes caught the "From" line of the message. CANNOT LIE CITIZEN BERLIN. His mind raced. "Look who sent this, Evie. 'Cannot lie' . . . Who was the famous character that could never tell a lie?"

Evie sighed. That was a story they'd known since they were tiny. "Cassandra," she said. "From Greek mythology. Grandma's favorite character. That's why she gave that name to —"

"To *Mom* — it's Mom's first name!" Andrew exclaimed. "And the next word — 'citizen'? Mom loves old movies. But what's her all-time favorite?"

"*Citizen Kane,*" Evie replied.

Kane. Mom's maiden name.

"The last word in the 'From' line is 'Berlin,' Evie. Like the Berlin Wall. Put them all together — go ahead."

Cannot lie Citizen Berlin.

In the reflected light of the monitor, Evie's slow smile seemed almost fluorescent. "Cassandra Kane Wall," she said.

Mom.

Totally Mom.

Andrew grabbed his universal key from his night-table drawer and raced for the door. He didn't stop running until he was down the stairs and in the garage.

Pop's key was still missing from the rack. "Look, Evie," he said, as his sister ran up behind him, "Pop didn't misplace his key. He *never* does that. Mom must have taken it, or hidden it. So Pop would have to leave the car . . . so we could follow her instructions!"

But Evie was already in the garage, wandering around, scanning the floor. She stopped, standing over a large footprint in a fresh pile of sand. Pop always put sand on oil spills, no matter how small. "This print is fresh. And huge. A man's sneaker. And don't tell me it's Pop. He *never* wears sneakers."

Andrew nodded confidently. "Yup. Just like you said, Mom couldn't be seen coming into the house. So she sent someone else. Someone who wouldn't be suspected."

"At three in the morning? Who *wouldn't* be suspected?"

But Andrew was already inserting the key into the trunk lock. It was too big to fit, so he dug his fingernails into the edge of the round key head, which was scored like the edge of a quarter.

It turned. Slowly the teeth of the key began to retract. Andrew tried the lock again, carefully, working the key head while jiggling the key to the right.

Click.

"Works every time," Andrew said.

The trunk squeaked open.

Inside, in full view, was a big, beautiful cardboard box.

Chapter Three

"These look *so* cool . . ." Andrew dug out a pair of sunglasses from the box in the trunk. He put them on, turning toward Evie. They were thick and heavy, like a contraption in an eye doctor's office. "Hey, they're X-ray vision! What's that say on your designer underwear? Giorgio *who?*"

Evie ducked behind the car. "*Stop!*"

"Just kidding. I can't see anything. They're the darkest sunglasses ever made. There are two pairs, in case you want to share the experience."

"I'll pass," Evie grumbled. "And that wasn't funny."

Andrew took the glasses off and pulled out a hard, felt-covered case. He snapped it open to reveal a gold-edged pen. "Awww . . . it's a belated birthday present," he said softly. "Mom knows I love pens."

"If Mom sent it, it must *mean* something," Evie reminded him. She pulled out a small canister labeled KODAK. "Thirty-five-millimeter film? Why would she give us this?"

"Maybe she doesn't know we went digital." Andrew took out the last and biggest item in the box — a heavy metal hook with a horizontal grip. "Cool. I've seen people opening sewer covers with these."

The idea of going into the sewers did not appeal to Evie at all. "Is there a note? That'll explain everything. Mom *always* leaves a note." She peeked inside the empty box, lifting the bottom flaps. She checked inside the trunk. Nothing in either place.

Andrew was tossing things into his backpack. "We have to examine all of it . . . take everything apart —"

"Later. Let's hide the box upstairs. If we don't leave in two minutes, we're going to be late for school."

As Evie and Andrew raced into first-period history at Adolph Green Middle School, their teacher sat at his desk, motionless, his face buried in papers. Mr. Fitzgerald had been teaching the same class for forty years. He liked to say (over and over) that he not only taught history, he'd lived history.

Most kids wished he *were* history.

Mr. Fitz didn't look up as kids yelled greetings and noisily settled in at their desks. His jet-black toupee glistened like a licorice helmet, a fringe of wispy (and much grayer) hair emerging from the bottom. He was wearing the same wool tweed jacket he'd worn all week.

Clink — clatter-clatter-clatter — clink, thump.

Rosie Moorehead followed Evie into the classroom, the trinkets on her backpack swinging noisily. Her unruly thatch of red hair bounced as she headed for a seat in the back.

Rosie's friend, Doreen Franklin, stepped in right behind her. "Well," she said, her lips pursed, "*I* have manners enough to say hello instead of stomping to the back of the room. Hello, Andrew and Evie!"

"Um, hi, Doreen," Evie said, eyeing the two girls curiously. Rosie and Doreen were best friends. Rosie had run Doreen's campaign for student presidency. "What's with you two?"

Doreen carefully appraised her freshly washed blond hair in the window of the classroom door, adjusting her black barrette until the look was just so. Everything about Doreen was just so. Evie still found it hard to believe that her parents were the Franklins, the tattooed hippie bikers and ex-Company members who worked with Mom.

Leaning in toward Andrew and Evie, Doreen whispered, "You see those little plastic thingies hanging from Rosie's pack — the spray bottles? She carries breath spray, deodorant spray, and bathroom spray . . . but that's not all. *Bear* spray, too. It's a kind of strong pepper spray. Can you believe it? Her mom makes her carry it in case she's ever attacked by a bear in the woods."

"You're mad at her, huh?" Andrew asked.

Doreen's eyebrows arched. "Mad? You don't know how it feels when your former best friend blows an election for you."

Rinnng!

At the class bell, Mr. Fitz looked up.

As Doreen pranced to her seat, Andrew and Evie scrambled into their theirs. Andrew sat behind Evie, one row to the left.

"We have, um, some very exciting news," Mr. Fitz said, his voice like the drone of a distant lawn mower. "As you know, we have been studying, er, the history of our uniquely situated and some say ill-fated metropolis, and as you know, uh, I believe that an adequate appreciation of history cannot be gained without ample enrichment from firsthand materials . . ."

Zzzzzz . . .

Barry Garf, who sat next to Evie, was already dozing.

"And so," Mr. Fitz droned on, "in our unit about San Francisco's troubled relationship with its penal institutions, I have arranged a field trip to the famous prison no one could escape —"

"Adolph Green Middle School," Doreen murmured.

"— Alcatraz Island," Mr. Fitz said.

Barry's eyes blinked open. "We're visiting Alcatraz? Cool!"

As the class erupted with comments and cheers, Evie smiled. Alcatraz Island *was* cool.

"Um . . . er . . . class?" Mr. Fitz said, adjusting his glasses, his eyes like a fish's staring through aquarium glass. "*Class?* Settle down, please!"

"Yes, class — settle down and take notes!" Andrew bellowed in a mock teacher voice. With a flourish, he took out Mom's fancy fountain pen and pretended to write. "Four score and seven years ago, we the people . . ."

A spitball whizzed by from left to right. "*Squawk! Squaawwwk! I am the Birdman of Alcatraz!*" someone cried out in the back of the class.

Bleeeeep! Bleeeeep!

Evie cringed. It was Andrew's cell phone. Another call for pizza.

"Oh, my . . ." Mr. Fitz muttered, his face reddening. "Oh, dear. *Harrumph.* Enough, kids! I will count to five — *one . . . two . . .*"

"Rats!" Andrew muttered. "The point won't come

down . . ." He held up his pen, repeatedly pressing the button at the top. *Click-click-click-click-click —*

Bleeeeep! Bleeeeep!

". . . *Five!*" In a sudden burst of life, Mr. Fitz stalked through the maze of desks and snatched the pen from Andrew's hand. "That's quite a catchy beat, Andrew, all that clicking and beeping . . ."

Andrew quickly turned off the phone. "Give me back the pen, it's a clue!"

Evie groaned, and covered her face with her hand.

"Clue? No, no, I'd say it's a Mont Blanc, circa 1969 or so. Where did you get such a fine antique?" Mr. Fitz examined the pen with admiration, slowly unscrewing it. As he pulled the two halves of the pen apart, Evie felt her heart jump.

A rolled-up sheet of bright yellow paper was jutting out of the pen's barrel.

A note.

Mom's note.

"Well, well, well," Mr. Fitz said, "you've been passing notes behind my back, eh?"

"Ooooooh," someone called out. "Busted!"

Andrew's face was bone white. "No. It's . . . it's . . ."

"A prescription!" Evie burst out.

"Oh?" As Mr. Fitz unrolled the paper, the class fell

stone silent. "Well, it looks like gibberish to me. Your . . . um, *doctor* should learn to use his handy little prescription pads. And you two should be ashamed of yourselves."

Grinning smugly, Mr. Fitz held the note over his trash can.

And then he tore it into shreds.

Chapter Four

"And so we see, um, regarding the rumors of, uh, vast underground escape routes from Alcatraz," Mr. Fitz said, moving slowly across the front of the classroom, "they were just that — er, rumors."

Evie hadn't heard a word Mr. Fitz had said all period. Her eyes were on the trash can.

The note was "gibberish," he'd said.

Great. Just great. That meant only one thing. It was a note from Mom, in code.

And now it was torn-up trash.

She peered around toward her brother. He was doodling on a sheet of loose-leaf. Across the top he had drawn the name ALCATRAZ, and under it a jail cell containing a screaming person with a striped shirt labeled A. WALL.

Big help.

RIINNGGG!

At the bell, kids who had been half asleep sprang to their feet and stampeded to the door.

Evie grabbed her books and spun around to Andrew. "*Get the pen — now,*" she whispered. "*I'll get the note.*"

Andrew looked startled for a moment. But then he quickly closed up his notebook, packed up, and shuffled to the front of the class, where Mr. Fitz was erasing the blackboard. "Excuse me . . . Mr. Fitz? I'd like my pen back, if you don't mind . . ."

"Oh?" Mr. Fitz said, giving him a sidelong glance.

Andrew planted himself between Mr. Fitz and the door, so the teacher's back was to Evie. "See, it's a long story, going back to, um . . . 1969 . . ."

Evie sidled silently up to the desk.

"It begins with my mom as a little girl," Andrew said. "Because of World War II, there was a shortage of pens in the land . . ."

"World War II ended in 1945," Mr. Fitz pointed out.

Andrew frowned. "I meant . . . the *Korean* War?"

Evie lunged for the trash can, pulling out the yellow strips of torn-up note, making sure to shove each one in her pocket.

"Try again, Andrew," Mr. Fitz said.

Done. Evie gave Andrew the thumbs-up and ran for the door.

"The *Gulf* War?" Andrew asked hopefully.

*   *   *

Evie tromped upstairs and dumped her backpack on her bed. "World War II?" she asked. "What were you thinking?"

"A diversionary tactic," Andrew said. "The best way to win someone's confidence is to make him think he's smarter than you."

Evie reached into her pocket and spilled the scraps of the note onto her desk. Andrew pulled up a chair, and they began to piece the fragments of the message together. Andrew held them down while Evie carefully taped them.

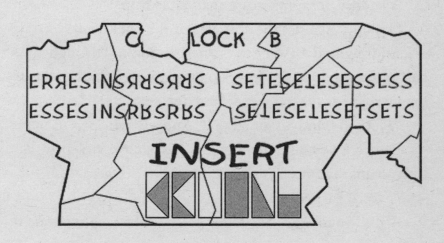

"Looks like some kind of alien language," Andrew said. "And what's with 'INSERT'? What are we supposed to insert?"

"At the top — CLOCK B . . ." Evie said. "That's got to be the key to solving this."

"If there's a Clock B, is there a Clock A and C?" Andrew volunteered.

"A clock store! It's another scavenger hunt, Andrew. We have to go to a clock store and find another clue — like we had to go to the record shop and the shoe store." Evie grabbed a San Francisco phone book from the neatly organized shelves beside her desk. "Clocks . . ." she said, riffling through the pages.

Sshhhhhhckkk.

A sudden scraping noise made her stop.

Outside. Against the shingles of the back wall.

Andrew and Evie both turned to look. Through the half-open window, the leaves on the overgrown backyard maple rustled.

"Is it . . . windy out today?" Andrew whispered.

Before Evie could answer, the tree shook violently, as if the trunk had been twanged by a giant finger.

A voice gasped.

A dull thud sounded from below. The tree was suddenly still.

Evie ran for the window and threw it open. Through the thick canopy of leaves, she and Andrew could see a dark figure disappear around the corner of the house.

"You take the front, I'll take the back!" she shouted, racing out of the room.

They barreled downstairs. As Andrew headed for the front door, Evie shot out the back.

At the base of the tree was a slight indentation in the grass and a couple of dropped candy wrappers.

Evie knelt to pick one up.

Andrew's footsteps sounded from the side of the house. "He's gone," he said breathlessly, running into the yard.

"It's not a he," Evie said softly. "Look what I found."

She held out the candy wrapper to her brother.

It was a Skor bar.

Andrew smiled. "Mom's favorite," he said.

Chapter Five

"Behold the Rock," Mr. Fitz shouted into a bullhorn, as the ferry approached Alcatraz across the choppy waters of San Francisco Bay.

A giant stone wart. That's what Alcatraz looked like to Andrew. A wart that had burst through the water's surface, with walls that seemed to rise from the stone itself.

He hated leaving the mainland. Mostly because water travel made him sick — but also because it meant leaving Mom behind. She was in San Francisco, no doubt about it now. He fingered the Skor bar wrapper in his pocket. Mom had been climbing their tree last night. How weird was *that?* Why had she done it? Mom was a high-tech sophisticated Company-trained spy. Climbing trees was Nancy Drew stuff.

"Imagine you are an Alcatraz prisoner — and somehow you've escaped, past the armed guards, the dogs, the fortified walls," Mr. Fitz barked. "You're free! Now all you have to do is get to the mainland. Sound easy?"

The ferry was hopping wildly on the currents. The

water was metallic gray, churning and whitecapped, as if monsters were having an undersea brawl. The plastic seats, the metal floor, everything around Andrew seemed to be made of liquid.

He did not like this feeling. Not one bit.

Mrs. Franklin, the parent chaperone for his and Evie's group, was sitting in front, wearing a tank top and humming sea chanteys under her breath. The long serpent tattooed across her shoulders seemed to undulate along with the tune.

Mrs. Franklin had been keeping a close eye on Andrew and Evie ever since her husband left to look for Mom.

"Look at this, Andrew," Evie said from the next seat, tilting an Alcatraz floor map toward him. "These guys lived like sardines."

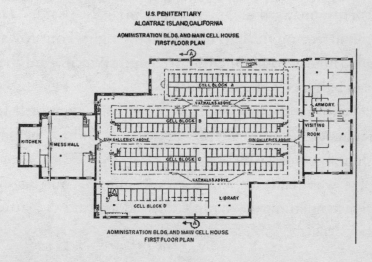

"Several men tried to make the swim," Mr. Fitz announced. "Two of them were carried away by currents toward the Golden Gate Bridge, and then out into the Pacific. Another, Jack Allen, was never heard from again. He was probably swallowed up by the raging currents."

"Yeah, right," said Barry Garf, who was sitting behind Andrew. "They escaped into those tunnels under Chinatown. Everyone knows that."

Mrs. Franklin turned around. "Rumors, Barry. Urban legends. Those tunnels were proven false ages ago. Now stop talking, please, and pay attention."

Andrew tried to ignore the discussion. The mention of tunnels — and the thought of the cramped-looking Alcatraz cells — did not help his stomach. He hated tight spaces almost as much as he hated travel by boat.

"How many did they squeeze in?" Evie said. "Let's see. Fourteen on the left, fifteen on the right. Four rows of twenty-nine across! One hundred and sixteen. And that's just in half a cell block. Look!"

She thrust the map in front of him. The tight little rectangular cells swam before his eyes. "*Gurp,*" he said, pushing the map aside.

He was ready to run for the railing — but his eyes caught something he hadn't noticed before. A pattern.

The rectangles began to settle, and so (miraculously) did his stomach.

"Are you okay?" Evie asked.

"Cell . . . block . . ." Andrew murmured. He took out the taped-together message and held it next to the map. *Evie, that's it!*

"What's it?"

"*Shh!* We have to be quiet," he hissed, looking around. "Okay. I think I know what the key to Mom's message is! Look at the top!"

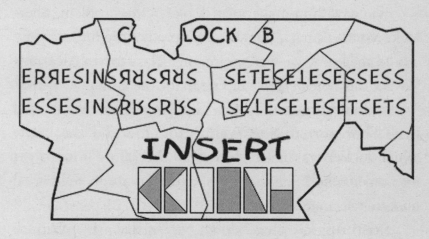

"Clock B," Evie said.

"Not CLOCK. It couldn't be the word CLOCK — because there are *letters missing*. Letters between the C and the LOCK were ripped out. That scrap probably got buried in the trash can, under the remains of Mr. Fitz's breakfast or something. This has to be a longer word or a phrase." Andrew held up the Alcatraz map. "Look. Look closely."

Evie's face slowly brightened. "*Cell Block B . . .*"

"*That's* what Mom meant," Andrew whispered. "And look at the arrangement of cells in Cell Block B. Two parallel rows on the left, and two on the right! Just like the nonsense letters in Mom's note — the letters that are above the word INSERT. What if we insert the letters into the Alcatraz jail cells on the map?"

Evie gave him a skeptical look. "One problem, Sherlock. Mom is smart, but she can't predict the future. How would she know we were going on a class trip to Alcatraz? We got this note *before* Mr. Fitz made the announcement."

Andrew shrugged. "How did Mom know we moved from Shoreport to San Francisco? How did she know which locker was mine? How did she know how to get into our garage? She's a spy. She just *knows*." He handed his sister the map and the note. "You do it. I'll get seasick."

"Real spies," Evie said, "do not hurl." With a mechanical pencil, she carefully copied the letters into the cells of Cell Block B:

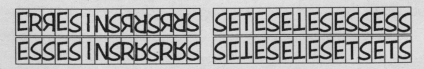

"Now what?" she said. "It's the same message, only in boxes. Big whoop."

Andrew could feel the ferry swinging around, backing into the dock. Mrs. Franklin, who had gone to the railing to watch, now came back to her group. "Okay, guys. Up and at 'em — and if you're not well-behaved, we lock you and leave you." She laughed at her own joke.

"*Mo-o-o-om*," Doreen said, looking embarrassed.

"*I* thought that was very funny, Mrs. Franklin," Rosie said, rising from a seat in the middle of the deck. She shuffled off to the exit ramp, her backpack hangs clanking behind her.

As the class headed toward a cramped cement entrance corridor, Andrew moved with the crowd, not looking up. He felt much better on solid ground, and he had his eye on the part of the note he still couldn't figure out:

INSERT.

Evie had already inserted the letters into the cells. What were the shapes for? Were *those* supposed to be inserted, too?

Six shapes, he thought. *All different.*

Six shapes. And six letters in the word INSERT.

"The prisoners had a rather Spartan visiting room," Mr. Fitz was saying, "a large mess hall, and a . . . less-than-luxurious library."

Andrew looked up to see a decrepit, dingy room with peeling paint and a few broken bookshelves against a radiator. But his mind was on the code, not on Alcatraz. The shapes — they were the key. Evie had put the *letters* into the cells. But that wasn't right. It should have been the *shapes.*

As he walked with the crowd, following whoever was closest, he took out a pencil and began erasing Evie's letters, then replacing them — the shape under the letter I for each I, the shape under the letter N for each N . . .

He was vaguely aware of someone — Barry, maybe — telling him to take a seat, and he lowered himself onto a hard bench. His cell phone bleeped, but he ignored it. No time for pizza orders now.

The drawing took a long time. A very long time.

When he had finally replaced the last letter, he leaped up. "*I've got it!*"

His voice resounded hollowly. The class was gone.

A striped shadow fell across the room. A rusty toilet seat, open and lopsided, was behind him. He turned toward the only source of light and saw the thick iron bars of a locked cell door.

"Hello?" he called out. "Um, is this a joke?"

No answer.

He grabbed the bars and pushed. They did not move.

The bare, rough walls seemed to close in from both sides. In the distance he heard the sound of a ferry motor.

"Oh, no . . ." he said, his voice parched and raw. "*NO-O-O-O-O-O!*"

Chapter Six

"*WARDEN!*" Andrew screamed, his breaths shallow, his head light. "*SOMEONE . . . GET ME OUT OF HERE!*"

The first sputter came from the left.

It was followed by a giggle from the right. And then a big guffaw — Barry's — that caused an explosion of uncontrollable laughter.

"N-n-not funny!" Andrew cried, wiping the sweat from his forehead.

"*What on earth are you doing?*" Mrs. Franklin's voice bellowed.

She appeared in front of the cell door and gave it a solid push. It swung open with a loud, rusty creak. "All of you are in deep, deep doodoo," she told Barry and his friends.

Andrew slunk out of the cell, shaking.

The other groups were clattering up the stairs now. Led by Evie.

She took her brother's arm. "'*Warden*'?" she

whispered. "You embarrass me sometimes. Are you all right?"

Andrew nodded. "M-Mom's code . . . I solved it."

"Really? Let me see!"

Before Andrew could hand it over, Mr. Fitz came trudging up the stairs. "Andrew, was that you?"

"Yes, sir." Andrew stuffed the code solution in his pants pocket.

"He needs room — *lots* of room," Evie announced. "He's seriously claustrophobic."

"Take him into one of the big rooms for a few moments," Mr. Fitz suggested. "Then meet us downstairs. We'll be watching a historical film."

Mrs. Franklin gave Evie a suspicious glance.

"This happens all the time," Evie assured her. "He'll feel more comfortable in a minute."

As the class walked away, Evie pulled Andrew into a cavernous, dusty room with a few long tables. "Show me what you did."

"The letters you wrote in the cells — I realized they were the same letters contained in the word 'insert': I, N, S, E, R, and T," Andrew said, pulling the sheet out of his pocket. "And I noticed each letter had its own funny little rectangular shape. So I filled the *shapes* into the cells, instead of the *letters*."

Evie nodded. "And where the R is upside down, the shape is upside down . . ."

"Or flipped, or whatever. Like this."

Andrew carefully unfolded the solved code:

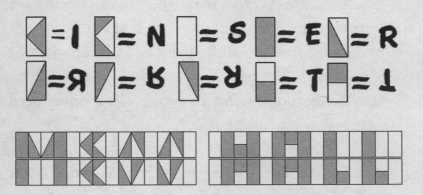

"You did all that? But you have no artistic skills."

"*Just read it, Evie!*"

"Read what? I see four lines of weird artwork."

"Hold it at a distance and look at the whole thing. They're letters. Chopped in half. Imagine the top half and the bottom stuck together."

Evie's eyes grew as wide as baseballs. "*Mess hall . . .* Andrew, that's . . ."

Andrew smiled. "Right here."

Evie looked around at the empty, decrepit room. Every window ledge was covered with a dark coat of dust. The floor was decorated with piles of chipped paint. Rusted radiators stood neglected against the walls. Far in the back was a lone sink, small and stained. "This is disgusting," she said. "They *ate* here? They all washed their hands in one dirty sink? I don't get this, Andrew. What are we supposed to find here? Was there another part to the note?"

Andrew's phone bleeped again.

"*Will you shut that thing off?*" Evie demanded.

Andrew fished his phone out of his pocket. The screen was lit up with words. "Hey . . . it's not a pizza order. It's a text message. Look."

For unruly skin:
Hot hot cold
Cold hot cold
Cold hot

"An ad." Evie began snooping around the room, examining graffiti. "There's hope. Maybe someday you'll get a message from a real person."

In the distance, from downstairs, Andrew could hear the sound of a movie announcer's voice. Before long, Mrs. Franklin and Mr. Fitz would be wondering where they were. They'd have to move fast.

"There has to be some other clue," Evie said. "Something carved into a table or drawn on the wall? Something left behind the radiator or in the sink?"

"Wait a minute . . ." Andrew said, still staring at the cell phone screen. "'*Unruly skin*' — it's a code, Evie! A scrambled-word code. One word is altered, and the other tells you what to do. Like when Mrs. Digitalis — er, Foxglove — wrote 'backward ETA.' That meant, 'spell ETA backward' — 'ate.'"

Evie nodded. "Or like 'mixed-up cat.' You could mix up the letters to make 'act.'"

"Exactly. Unruly skin. Something unruly is something mixed up. So if you mix up the letters of 'skin,' you get . . ."

Before he finished they'd both dashed to the sink.

It had a small sloping porcelain basin, stained green-blue by water that had probably stopped running decades ago. Andrew crouched, examining the pipes that ran from under the sink and into the wall. Around the pipes, where they entered the wall, was a large rectangular cut.

"A trapdoor," Andrew said.

Evie knelt next to him, wrapping her fingers around the pipes. "This is shut tight."

Andrew eyed a round metal ring that jutted out from one of the pipes. He unhooked his backpack, took out the grappling hook, and inserted it into the ring. "Perfect fit."

He gave the hook a strong yank, but it didn't budge.

"Let me try." Evie elbowed him aside and held the hook herself. Propping her foot against the wall, she pulled and pulled.

Andrew stared once again at the cell phone screen: FOR UNRULY SKIN: HOT HOT COLD/COLD HOT COLD/COLD HOT.

Evie was grunting and pulling so hard that the sink was beginning to shake. Its faucets wobbled, loose on their metal threads.

Faucets.

Hot and cold faucets!

Andrew leaned over his sister and grabbed the HOT knob. As he turned, it gave a piercing squeak.

"What are you doing?" Evie asked.

"Turning the knobs — like the message said!"

Hot . . . hot . . . cold. Cold . . . hot . . . cold. Cold . . . hot. As he turned the knobs in order, they squeaked like a chatty family of rats.

"Okay, Evie, *now!*" Andrew said.

Evie pulled again.

The sink, along with the rectangular section of the wall, swung out heavily on a hinge. The grappling hook clanked onto the floor, and Evie fell on her back.

Behind the opening was a hole, a hollowed-out wall that plunged to darkness.

"Open sesame," Andrew whispered.

Chapter Seven

"Hello?" Andrew shouted into the void. "What are we supposed to do — drop down in there with our Jedi blasters and liquid-cable spike launchers?"

"What?" Evie said.

"Never mind." Andrew peeked over the edge. It was pitch-black. And, judging from Evie's echo, very deep. His stomach did a flip-flop. "Sh-she can't expect us to, like, *jump* . . . can she?"

"We should have brought a flashlight," Evie said. "We were stupid."

"How were we to know? Mom didn't warn us. In her note she didn't say, 'Bring a flashlight.' She should have told us instead of just leading us to a black hole."

"Great, Andrew. That's really nice. Blame Mom." Evie picked up the grappling hook from the floor and dropped it into Andrew's backpack.

It made a loud clank.

"Evie . . . what was that?" Andrew asked.

Evie shrugged glumly. "Star Wars hardware? That would be my guess."

Andrew took the backpack and looked inside. It wasn't hardware. The hook had clanked against the two pairs of sunglasses.

He reached inside and pulled one out. It was bulky and strange — and much more complex-looking than he'd first noticed in the garage. There were tiny gauges along the arms, and a switch labeled NV on the right side. "What's NV?" he asked.

"Nino Valenti . . . *the designer?*" Evie said in disbelief. "Those are Nino Valentis?"

Andrew flipped the switch, put on the glasses, and looked into the square opening. It was no longer black. He could see a grayish wall, painted with an arrow pointing down. "Night Vision," he said. "They're *night-vision glasses*, Evie! Infrared. Whatever. Put yours on. Flip the switch on the right side."

As he leaned into the hole, Evie crowded next to him, adjusting her glasses. Below them, a sturdy ladder led downward through a narrow passage in the wall that glowed dully in a thousand gradations of greenish-gray. A distant red circle, like a blood stain, marked the bottom.

Andrew felt dizzy and numb. "W-we're supposed to g-go down there?"

"You can't let a little claustrophobia stand in the way of finding Mom," Evie said firmly. "Go ahead. I'll be right above you."

"*Me* first?"

"That way you won't be able to chicken out."

Sweat pooled at the base of Andrew's neck. Evie had him tightly by the arm. She was counting on him. *Mom* was counting on him. Mom could be down there, just out of sight. Waiting.

"If I die, will you tell Pop good-bye?" he asked.

"*Just go* — before Mr. Fitz and Mrs. Franklin come and find us!"

Andrew stepped gingerly over the lip of the hole. His legs shook as he forced them to go downward — slowly, rung by rung, over fifty of them before he lost count. Below him, the red circle loomed larger and larger, until finally he stepped onto it solidly.

"That wasn't so bad, was it?" Evie whispered, stepping down next to him.

It was bad. It was very bad — warm and stuffy and hard to breathe. The air was thick with the smell of mildew and seaweed. His legs felt like taffy. A long, narrow tunnel stretched out before them, disappearing around a bend. "Well. No one here. Let's go back."

He grabbed the ladder, but Evie pulled him away. "We just started," she said. "Let's look down that tunnel."

Andrew gulped. On an ordinary day, he would not have been caught dead holding his sister's hand. Now he clutched it tightly as they crept along.

The tunnel arched over them in a semicircle, the apex just inches above their heads. If Andrew moved his head, the NV glasses made the walls grow and shrink like a funhouse mirror, so he struggled to keep looking straight ahead. His and Evie's footsteps were nearly silent on the dirt floor as they padded along the tunnel's sweeping curve, always seeming to head slightly downhill. Andrew had to keep swallowing so his ears wouldn't clog. "We must be underwater," he said.

"*Shh,*" Evie replied.

It felt like miles. Kilometers. Whichever was longer. Andrew figured they were halfway to Texas by the time the tunnel finally began to widen. And soon they were walking into a chamber — four unmarked walls, no furniture. At the far end of the chamber was a closed door.

"Evie, this is creepy," Andrew said. "This is soooo creepy."

Click.

They both froze as the door slowly swung open.

A light went on. The brightness was harsh, knifelike. Andrew ripped off his glasses. He squinted, his eyes adjusting. Two people were stepping into the room now, a man and a woman. They were smiling. Neither of them was Mom.

"They made it," the man said.

"I told you they were smart," the woman replied.

"Who are you?" Evie demanded. "And where's our mom?"

"I'm Spy N and this is Spy O," the woman said with a laugh. "Very cloak-and-dagger, I know. Sorry, we didn't choose the code names. And your mother, you'll both be happy to know, is very close. You can relax now. You will be seeing her soon. That is precisely why you're here."

The man, Spy O, gestured for them to follow him into the next room. "Come on," he said, his voice gruff and low.

"She's in *there?*" Andrew asked, eyeing the two spies nervously.

"Don't you want to see her?" the guy asked.

"Yes!" Evie exclaimed. "But . . . why won't she come out of the room?"

"Oh, it's not a room," Spy N said with a smile. "It's a tunnel. A long one — leads all the way to the city, under the bay."

"We're not at the city yet?" Andrew asked.

"Quite a way from it," Spy N replied. "The convicts began building this tunnel, as you might expect — but you can't get very far scraping with stolen spoons. During the Cold War, our people took over construction on a more professional scale. When the Transbay Tube was being built to transport cars under the bay, we . . . *diverted* some of the construction equipment. The San Francisco fog helped our secrecy, of course. At that time everyone thought Alcatraz was abandoned. In reality, we had set up a training facility here. Once agents were ready, they would be transferred to our base of West Coast operations, an ancient network of tunnels under Chinatown. We call it Minotaur."

"But I thought those tunnels under Chinatown were rumors," Evie said. "Everybody says so."

"That's because we planted rumors of our own," the woman explained. "Rumors that the tunnels did *not* exist. Rumors of rumors. The most sophisticated people believed us, of course, so we were safe. Anyway, once we'd built Minotaur, training and operations were joined. We could travel between Alcatraz and the mainland, unseen. Believe me, Evelyn, those tunnels are there, all right."

"Who's 'we'?" Evie asked. "Who are you, anyway?"

"We work with your mother," answered the man, Spy O. "Look, are you coming, or are we going to play twenty questions?"

Spy N tried to take Evie's hand, but she backed away. "We're with a school group. Kids don't just disappear from school groups. We'll be suspended. It'll be on our permanent records. Mom would never force us to do that. How do we know you're telling the truth? Where is Mom, anyway? Why isn't she here?"

Andrew swallowed hard. He felt short of breath. If there was one thing he feared more than a closed, stuffy tunnel, it was a *fight* in a closed, stuffy tunnel. He nudged his sister in the ribs. "Um, look, we really do want to see Mom, but I think what my sister means is . . . maybe you can just show us some ID? That's all. And then, maybe we could just wait here . . . while you page her. Or whatever."

"We're a secret organization," Spy O snapped. "You expect us to have ID? Let's go! Move!"

Spy N wheeled around to him and glared. "Gentle, Spy O. They have a right to ask questions."

"We don't have time!"

"They are children."

As the spies bickered in low voices, Evie sidled close to Andrew. "I don't trust them."

"But Mom sent us down here," Andrew reminded her, without much conviction in his voice. He wanted to get out of this room and go with them. How could he and Evie *not* follow Mom's clues?

Still, this was strange. This didn't seem like Mom's way of doing things.

Beads of sweat prickled Spy O's balding scalp, which shone dully in the fluorescent light. Something about him was familiar . . .

As the man argued with Spy N, he turned toward the twins. His scowling eyes met Andrew's dead-on before he turned back.

Andrew stiffened.

He'd seen the face before. In Foxglove's house. Stealing data from her computer. Snooping around in her living room.

He took Evie's hand and began backing away. "They're lying . . ." he whispered.

"How do you know?" Evie replied. "How *can* they be?"

"Details later. We split — *now!*"

He turned on his heels and ran, pulling Evie along with him.

"Come back!" Spy N cried out.

"GET THEM!" Spy O bellowed.

Andrew and Evie sprinted into the corridor, their footfalls dull in the soupy air. As the illumination from the chamber dimmed, they fumbled for their glasses, donning them on the run.

Uphill, the tunnel seemed longer. Andrew's legs were killing him. Behind him, the spies' footsteps were coming closer.

Evie reached the ladder first and began to climb. Andrew's sweaty hands slipped on the rung. He quickly wiped them on his pants, gripped the rungs, and began to haul himself up.

He had climbed three steps when Evie let out a sudden cry. Her back came smashing down into his face. He let go of the ladder and fell to the floor with a heavy thud.

His glasses flew away, landing in the dirt.

Evie shrieked. She was flailing, fighting against someone — or some*thing* — that had fallen from above. Andrew sprang to his feet, reaching into the blackness for his glasses.

"Help!" Evie cried. "*Andrew, help me!*"

There. Andrew's fingers closed around the glasses frame. As he slid them onto his face, a voice shouted: "*Freeze. I have bear spray!*"

Andrew couldn't believe his night-vision-enhanced eyes.

It was Rosie.

Chapter Eight

"*Got 'em!*"

Spy O's voice boomed through the tunnel. He was running toward the ladder, wielding a flashlight.

"Hold them there!" Spy N's voice cried from deeper within.

Evie was on the ground, the wind knocked out of her. Andrew backed against the wall, next to Rosie, who was huddled against the rock wall, staring sightlessly. She was holding a can of spray out in front of her.

Bear spray.

As Spy O lunged toward him, Andrew grabbed the can from Rosie's hand and aimed it at him.

"Hey, that's mine!" Rosie screamed.

TSSSSSSSS . . .

Spy O covered his face, gagging, staggering backward. Spy N was right behind him now. The spray hit her, too. Coughing violently, the two spies fell back into the corridor.

Andrew pulled his sister to her feet. "Can you walk?" he asked.

"I think so," Evie said, a little wobbly, adjusting her glasses.

"*Who stole my spray?*" Rosie screamed. "*What's going on here?*"

Andrew scooped Rosie's massive backpack off the ground, hooked it over his own, and pulled Rosie by the hand toward the ladder. "No questions. Just come on! Evie, get behind her. Make sure she doesn't do anything stupid."

Andrew took the rungs two at a time. With Rosie's pack and his aching legs, it felt like Mount Everest. At the top, the sink door was slightly ajar. He pushed it open with a gasp of agonized relief and tumbled into the room. After the tunnel, the mess hall felt like the Great Outdoors. Reaching into the hole, he helped Evie and Rosie climb out.

"*Ow* — my back!" Rosie complained. "I could sue you. My dad is a lawyer!"

"Fine, you do that," Evie shot back, catching her breath. "But when he asks where it happened, tell him the truth. You were trespassing illegally on private property. Because if you don't tell him, I will. *Just what were you doing there, anyway?*"

Rosie's mouth flapped open and shut. "It wasn't fair,"

she sputtered. "You got to sneak away from that boring movie downstairs. So I snuck away, too. You never talk to me anymore. Why have you guys been so mean to me? Huh? What did I do?"

"Never in my life have I thought a mean thing about you, Rosie," Evie said. "That is, until two minutes ago, when you nearly smothered me — *and you still haven't answered my question!*"

"You and Doreen," Rosie muttered, her face reddening, "you talk about me all the time. You pass secret notes. I saw. What was on that note, huh? What was *soooo* important that you had to take it out of the trash? *What did Doreen say about me?*"

Evie's jaw dropped like a stone. "The note in the pen — the one that Mr. Fitz ripped — you thought . . . ?"

"You followed us down there for *that?*" Andrew dropped Rosie's backpack to the floor. It fell open, spilling out books, magazines, pens, scraps of paper, small dolls, wrappers, and a shrink-wrapped packet of candy bars.

Skor bars.

At least a dozen of them.

Andrew gave his sister a look, but she seemed to have lost the capacity to speak. "Um, Rosie?" he said. "You didn't try to visit us last night — by way of the tree in our backyard, did you?"

"You guys were plotting against me!" Rosie said defensively. "You were talking on the phone with Doreen, weren't you?"

"*Whaaaat?*" Andrew and Evie said together.

"*Hello-o-o-o!*" Mrs. Franklin called into the mess hall. "Are you three conducting a self-guided tour?"

"Yes," Evie replied numbly, trudging toward the exit, "through the Twilight Zone. With our guide, Rosie."

Mrs. Franklin glanced suspiciously at their clothing. "How did you all get so dirty?"

Andrew shrugged, hooking his backpack onto his shoulders. "Guess that's why they call it a mess hall."

Chapter Nine

"Mrs. Franklin knows we were in the tunnel," Evie said. "The filthy clothes gave us away."

Andrew looked over her shoulder. School was finally over for the day, and they were already two blocks away from it. No one was following. It was safe to talk. "I'm not so sure, Evie. Your alibi was so good — that we were measuring the room for a report and had to crawl around on our hands and knees. Everybody bought it."

"Mrs. Franklin didn't. Look, Andrew — she works with Mom. So does her husband. Big-time spies like that are very smart."

Andrew shrugged. "So, that's good, right? We *want* her to know about the tunnel. Maybe she can explain what happened to us down there."

"Maybe . . ."

Evie's thoughts were tumbling around in her head as they slowly climbed the steep hill toward Jackson Street. She barely noticed the whiff of warm cherry pie from the

Pacific Heights Pastry Shop, or the lush smells from the open door of Flora's Flowerpot.

Mom had sent them clues to find the tunnel . . . but hadn't met them there. Instead, they found two people who claimed to work with her, and one of them was Spy O — the guy who had tried to capture Foxglove. He was, by definition, Mom's enemy.

What was he doing there? Was he a double agent, infiltrating Mom's people?

Or was he really a good guy now, a defector truly working with Mom? People did change sides sometimes.

Or was the whole thing a setup — a trap by The Company? They'd intercepted Mom's secret notes and captured the tunnel — and her — and now they wanted Andrew and Evie.

"I just don't know," Evie said. "I don't know what to believe anymore, or who to trust."

"But we *know* Mrs. Franklin's on our side," Andrew pointed out.

"Then why do I feel like we shouldn't talk to her? I'm just so confused, Andrew. And scared. Really scared. I wish we had someone to talk to that we *knew*. Someone whose advice we can trust. Like Mom or . . ."

Evie's voice trailed off.

"Or Pop?" Andrew said, pausing for the red light on Broadway.

"Yeah. Pop would know what to do. Sometimes I wish we didn't have to keep this a secret from him."

The light changed, and they began to walk. "Maybe we don't," Andrew said.

"We have to. Mom gave us instructions —"

"But that was a long time ago. Pop was being tailed. Mom had to keep him in the dark, to protect him. The idea was, no one suspected us. We were her best chance. But not anymore. Don't you see, Evie? Pop and us — we're in the same boat. What's the point in keeping secrets?"

"Mom sent *us* the box, not Pop," Evie said. "Mom hid Pop's keys so he wouldn't know. *She didn't want him to know, Andrew.*"

"But obviously something went wrong today," Andrew replied. "Those two goons figured out Mom's plan to meet us. Did you really think they were legit? They're the enemy, Evie! They could have hurt us! And what if they've kidnapped Mom? *How can we keep that from Pop?*"

"But . . . but she told us . . ." Evie sputtered, the conviction draining from her voice.

Andrew exhaled. "Look, I say we either talk to Mrs. Franklin or to Pop. One or the other. Take your pick. We can't do this alone anymore."

Andrew's words were sinking in. He was right. She *hated* to admit it, but Andrew had a point. A spy had to be smart. But a spy also had to be flexible.

"Okay," she said, as they made the turn onto Jackson. "I choose Pop. But let me do the talking."

Their house was a four-story red brick Victorian, with a narrow driveway that sloped steeply downward. Pop had taken the car to work — he'd discovered his keys hidden between the cushions of the basement sofa — but as Evie and Andrew walked up the stoop, Evie noticed the car through the windows of the garage. He was home early.

Pop was never home early. Except in emergencies.

"Uh-oh," Andrew muttered.

Evie slowly pushed open the front door. "Pop?" she called out.

"Come in here, please." Pop's voice called out from the living room.

Evie gulped. She and Andrew trudged through the dark, polished-oak archway that framed the biggest room in the house. Pop was still in his business suit, sitting on a red leather sofa across from two empty armchairs. A cup of black coffee steamed on a small glass table, over a patterned rug he had bought in Turkey. Evie noticed a new cord of wood had been stacked by the fireplace. Everything looked cozy, except for the expression on Pop's face.

As Andrew and Evie sank into the armchairs, Pop took a slow sip. "Cutting classes to gallivant around town a couple of weeks ago was bad enough," he said. "Being mean to Marisol and causing her to disappear without a trace was worse. But wandering off during a field trip?" Pop shook his head. "Your teacher, Mr. Fritz, was very upset. I didn't know what to say to him."

"Fitz," Andrew said meekly.

Evie gave her brother a glance, hoping for some moral support, but he looked like a penguin facing an avalanche. "Pop," she said carefully, "we didn't gallivant, we weren't mean to Marisol, and we didn't wander off. The truth is . . . well, we've been keeping something from you. Something very important."

Pop stared back at her blankly.

"See, Mom's been in touch with us." The words spilled out in a rush of fear and relief, faster than Evie could think. She told him about the boxes in Connecticut and San Francisco, about Foxglove, about the secret tunnel under Alcatraz and the nasty pair who had met them there. And all the while Pop listened silently, sipping coffee without so much as a nod.

"Look," Andrew finally piped up, "we weren't supposed to tell you this. Mom told us not to. But don't be mad at her. She had good reasons."

"We're just . . . scared, Pop," Evie said. "We need you."

Her words hung in the air with the scent of coffee and aging wood. Pop twirled his cup in his hand but didn't drink. His eyes seemed fixed on something deep in the black liquid.

When he spoke at last, his voice was soft and measured. "Thank you, Evie. And Andrew. Thank you both very, very much for having the bravery to say that. But I'm not as clueless as you think."

Andrew and Evie exchanged a startled glance.

"You . . . you *know?*" Evie said.

Pop nodded. "I, too, have been on the case about Mom. And like you, I will not rest until I find her."

Evie's legs pushed her out of her seat before her brain could give the command, and she was in Pop's lap, hugging him, crying. "Oh, Pop — I'm so glad . . . this has been so hard."

Andrew was standing over them, beaming. "We can do this," he said. "With you helping us, there's no stopping us!"

Pop managed a small smile, but Evie noticed his face

was still pensive, faraway. "Is something wrong, Pop?" she asked.

"Well, I have news, too," Pop said, "and it's something I'm not sure you're prepared to hear."

Evie and Andrew both sank back into their seats.

"Your mother," he said, "was involved in high-level international government business for years —"

"The Company," Andrew said. "We know."

"The Company is known for its secrecy," Pop continued. "And its complexity — businesses paying off governments, governments paying off businesses to pay off other businesses to pay off governments. . . . It's confusing. The rules, the legalities, are complex. It requires nerves — and morals — of steel. Even the strongest and smartest people are put to a severe test. You can get wrapped up in shady dealings that turn your head inside out. You lose track of who's good and who's bad, and after a while you can't help but think it doesn't make any difference. But it does. And that's the problem."

"We sort of knew that," Andrew said. "That's why Mom broke away, isn't it? Because she found out something shady about The Company?"

"Not exactly," Pop said.

"What are you saying, Pop?" Evie asked.

Pop took a slow, deep breath. "Under stress, sometimes

even the best people break. They do bad things and lie about them. They choose to run rather than suffer the consequences. Now, I know you think I'm compulsive and pushy, but the biggest part of my job is to protect you. To keep you from threats — even if the threat comes from someone very, very close."

"Close?" Evie said tentatively. "How close?"

Pop leaned forward, looking them both in the eye. "I didn't want to have to tell you this, kids," he said, "but if anyone isn't to be trusted, I'm afraid it's Mom."

Chapter Ten

Mom was the enemy.

Marisol was the good guy.

The world was upside down.

Mom wasn't *protecting* Pop. She was keeping him in the dark. Fooling him.

Fooling Andrew and Evie, too.

Fooling The Company.

Fooling the government.

Pop had told them everything he knew. The whole story. He'd known about Foxglove, back in Connecticut. He'd seen that her house had been ransacked. He'd seen Andrew and Evie in her car, when she was being chased by The Company. He hadn't been able to tail them, but after a few urgent phone calls to people in high places, he'd found out what had happened. Andrew remembered — just moments after Foxglove had ditched the car and hopped onto a moving train, Pop had pulled up behind them. At the time, Andrew hadn't thought to ask how Pop had tracked them down that evening.

Now Andrew knew. Pop had been on the case. That night, once Andrew and Evie were safe, Pop had requested an immediate transfer. A clean break. That was why they'd split to San Francisco so fast.

It was Mom. Mom had moved to the dark side.

Andrew hadn't slept all night. He and Evie had somehow managed to get to school this morning, but concentration was impossible. He felt as if he no longer had use of his feet and instead was being propelled from classroom to classroom, street to street, on automatic pilot.

Bombardier A. Wall . . . Galactic Commander Anakin Wall-P-5-Q-2 — neither of his favorite alter egos could help him now. He didn't even bother trying.

After school Evie met him in the hallway on the way to their lockers. "Cheer up," she said.

"That is *so* not the right thing to say right now," Andrew replied.

"Pop could be wrong," Evie reminded him.

"Pop is never wrong," Andrew replied.

"Look, he doesn't work for The Company, right? He works for another branch of the government. Remember Mom and Pop's old joke over dinner?"

Andrew nodded. "She says, 'How was work?' and he

says, 'I could tell you, but I'd have to shoot you.' I always hated that. They thought it was so funny."

"The point is, they never talked about work — because they had to keep secrets. Their branches of government rarely talk to one another."

"So how did Pop find out?" Andrew asked.

"I asked him, while you were brushing your teeth this morning . . ." They rounded the corner to a hallway full of lockers, where kids were yanking out books, slamming doors, saying loud good-byes. Evie leaned closer to her brother. "Declassified reports, he said. Word of mouth. Don't you see? It's not direct. It's not *firsthand* evidence that Mom is a traitor. What if The Company's trying to hide something? What if Mom really did find out about corruption, or whatever — would The Company send out a *truthful* report to other branches of government? Would they admit that Mom outed them? No way. They'd try to make *her* look bad."

"So you think Pop was *fooled?*" Andrew asked, a tiny sprig of hope sprouting in his brain.

Andrew stopped at his locker and opened it. A folded piece of paper floated to the floor.

"A love note from Rosie?" Evie said.

"Probably a notice of suspension for phoning in the whole day," Andrew grumbled, picking it up off the floor.

He unfolded it and read:

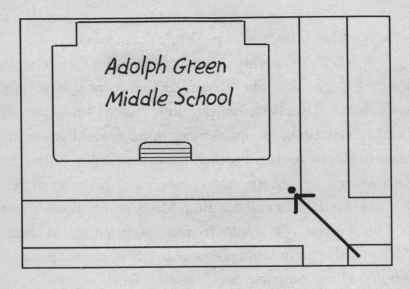

19 (US ⟶ WWII)

"Mom . . ." Evie said.

Andrew nodded. He knew he was supposed to be thrilled, but somehow he couldn't scrape together the excitement. "What should we do?"

"What do you mean?" Evie said excitedly. "Solve the code, of course!"

"What if it's another trap?"

Evie took her brother's chin between her thumb and forefinger and forced him to look her in the eye. "There are some people you have to trust, Andrew. If you don't, there's no point in anything at all."

Andrew heaved a big sigh. He held up the note again. "The arrow points to the corner," he said.

In minutes they were at the southeast corner of the school. The sounds of an Ultimate Frisbee game rang out from the lawn, and a score of kids were yakking on cell phones as they crossed the street. Next to the streetlight stood a battery of newspaper vending machines: *San*

Francisco Chronicle . . . Bay Area Bulletin . . . Oakland Gazette . . . New York Times . . . Wall Street Journal . . .

The last box was yellow and unmarked.

Inside, through a scratched Plexiglas window, Evie could see a package wrapped in plain brown paper. A padlock held the door tight.

"It's a combo lock," Andrew said, cupping it in his hands. "We won't be able to use our key."

"Maybe we don't need to," Evie said. "Look at the note!"

Andrew took the message from his pocket and looked at the first clue:

$$19 \ (US \longrightarrow WWII)$$

" 'Us arrow World War Two' . . ." he mumbled.

"You are losing your edge," Evie said. "How about United States, not *us*. United States going to World War Two. When did that happen?"

"We haven't read that chapter. Was it before or after the Civil War . . . ?"

"Nineteen forty-one!" Evie said. "*I* pay attention in class. Okay, that's the answer to the first question — forty-one! Now, question two . . ."

49

"The forty-nine tree . . ." Andrew said. "Four nine roots . . ."

"*Yes!*" Evie said.

"Yes what?"

"Think, Andrew — what's forty-nine?"

"Pop's age?"

"It's a perfect square! The *root* of forty-nine is *seven!* Okay, first clue forty-one, second clue seven. Next?"

They both stared at the last question:

"Blocks?" Evie said. "Ice?"

"It's a three . . ." Andrew muttered. "Cubed! The cube of three is nine!"

"No, the *square* of three is nine. The cube of three is twenty-seven."

"Right!" Andrew took a pen from his pocket and wrote the three answers down at the bottom of the message:

41 7 27

Evie grabbed the combination lock and spun it to forty-one . . . seven . . . twenty-seven . . .

Click.

The lock fell open. Evie swung the door down.

Andrew reached in and pulled out the brown box. It was heavy.

In Mom's handwriting across the top, it said CONGRATULATIONS.

Chapter Eleven

"A fingerprinting kit?" Andrew said, pulling out a pack that contained a magnifying glass, fingerprint powder, and a booklet entitled *Reading Fingerprints*. "Why?"

Sprawled out on her bed, Evie was examining a map on thick, sturdy paper. "This is a decent map of San Francisco. Just the north section, though. We have a million of these. Why would Mom think we *need* this?"

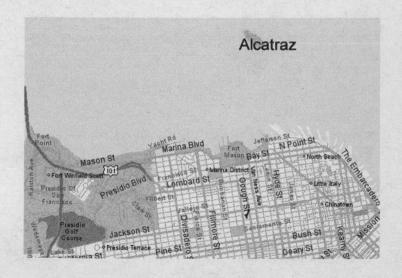

"There's a check mark in the middle. Maybe that means something." Andrew was trying in vain to unscrew a long, clunky-looking felt-tip pen. "I guess there are no messages hidden in this thing." He uncapped it and began writing on a sheet of paper. "It doesn't work, either."

With a shrug, Evie reached into the box and took out a transparent sheet. This one made no sense at all:

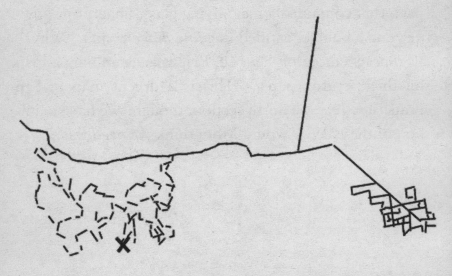

"Any idea what this is?" Evie asked.

"It's a triceratops," Andrew said. "I think Mom saved that from my preschool art class."

"Ha-ha," Evie said.

Andrew scooped a sheet of paper off the bottom of the box. His eyes narrowed. "Evie, what's this mean?"

She swung herself across the bed and looked over her brother's shoulder:

MARK BRICK WAS RUNNING A CHECK AT THE BLUE TAILED YANK. YOU WILL LOOK OUT FOR IT CLOSELY. BE SMART.

Today's lucky numbers:

4 3 20 12 13
19 10 18 7 8
6 1 14 16 5
9 2 11 17 15

"Do we know a Mark Brick?" she asked. "Or a place called the Blue-Tailed Yank?"

"Sounds very San Francisco. I'll do a quick search." Andrew swung around to his computer. His fingers clattered across the keyboard. "Hmmm . . . no one by that name in this state — and Google comes up blank on the Yank. It looks like a note Mom wrote to herself and dropped into the box by accident. Like, a reminder. With lottery numbers."

"Mom doesn't play the lottery!" Evie took the note and examined it carefully. "Those numbers must be the key. But what do they mean? Are they, like, a pattern?"

"I hate math," Andrew said.

"Four, three, twenty, twelve . . ." Evie shook her head. "No, they don't make any sense. What about substituting letters? Maybe if we replace 1 with A, 2 with B . . ."

She took a pen from the night table and began writing.

D E T L M
L J R G H

"Guess not," she said.

"I've got it!" Andrew exclaimed, grabbing the pen. "It's simple. We connect the numbers, in order, to form a shape that will make everything clear!"

Today's lucky numbers:

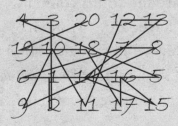

"Brilliant," Evie said drily.

Andrew began erasing the lines. "Three strikes, we're out."

"Maybe not." Evie gave the note a long, hard look. Words and numbers. She remembered the long code from Mom's first box. It had seemed impossible to break — even to get a handle on. Only when they numbered the words did the final solution become clear.

Picking up a pencil, she carefully wrote numbers under each word.

MARK BRICK WAS RUNNING A CHECK AT THE BLUE TAILED YANK.
  1   2   3   4   5 6 7 8 9   10   11
YOU WILL LOOK OUT FOR IT CLOSELY. BE SMART.
  12 13 14   15 16 17 18   19   20

Andrew's eyes brightened. "The lottery numbers — they go from one to twenty! So if we substitute the words for the numbers . . ."

Evie was already writing:

Today's lucky numbers:

4	3	20	12	13	RUNNING WAS SMART YOU ARE
19	10	18	7	8	BEING TAILED CLOSELY AT THE
6	1	14	16	5	CHECK MARK LOOK FOR A
9	2	11	17	15	BLUE BRICK YANK IT OUT

"'Running was smart . . .'" Evie read. "She *knows*, Andrew! She knows what happened to us — and she says we were right to run away!"

"'You are being tailed closely,'" Andrew continued reading. "'At the check mark, look for a blue brick. Yank it out.' What's *that* supposed to mean?"

"The check mark on the map she gave us!" Evie handed Andrew the map of San Francisco. In the midst of it, on a block near their neighborhood, was a small red check. "It's on Pacific, right near Franklin."

From downstairs came a rustling sound and the thump of the front door. "Kids? Are you here?"

Andrew shoved the paper into his pocket. *"Why is he always coming home early?"*

"Andrew, what do we do? Should we tell him?"

"No! I mean, yes. I mean, *I don't know.* We're supposed to be in this together —"

"Are we?" Evie asked. "I mean, he really believes Mom went over to the Dark Side. If we let him help us, he's going to turn Mom in."

"But she's his wife," Andrew said. "Would he — ?"

"You heard what he said. Look, maybe he's right. Maybe Mom made a mistake. Maybe she did something bad. But don't you want to see her first? Don't you want to hear her side of the story?"

Pop's heavy footsteps bounded up the stairs. "Heyyyy, what's going on up there — high-level secrets?"

Evie packed up the box and shoved it under the bed. Andrew quickly folded up the coded message and the map and put it in his back pocket. "Hi, Pop," Andrew called out.

Pop poked his head in the door. "You guys want an early dinner? My turn to cook."

"Pop, you look really tired," she said. "I think we should go out for dinner tonight. Like, maybe that new Italian restaurant, Il Duomo?"

"Wendy's is closer," Andrew piped up.

Evie shot him a poisonous glance. "You know, Pop, the one near *Franklin and Pacific?*"

"Oh . . ." Andrew murmured.

Pop scratched his head. "Do I look that bad? You know, it does sound like a good idea, Evie. I was up nearly all night on a project. Give me three minutes." He looked at his watch. "We'll meet downstairs at seventeen-eleven hours?"

Seventeen-eleven hours. That was military time for 5:11 P.M. "AOK," Evie replied.

Even during the early bird special at Il Duomo, when the kitchen had barely opened, the smell of tomato sauce and garlic was overpowering. "I'll have the *fusilli duomo* with shiitake mushrooms and the bolognese sauce with capers and shallots," Evie said to the waiter, handing over her menu.

"Spaghetti and meatballs," Andrew said.

Evie scowled at him. "Can't you ever get anything different?"

"It's the only thing on the menu I can pronounce."

Suddenly Andrew grimaced, pulling back from the table. They had planned the strategy for finding the message, flipping a coin to see who would get to leave the table and sneak out of the restaurant. Andrew had won, which was a good thing, because he was the better actor. He clutched his stomach and cast a longing glance toward the men's room. "All these smells are giving me a tummy-ache. May I be excused?"

Pop looked up with sudden concern. "We can eat at a Wendy's if you'd rather."

"I'll . . . be fine," Andrew said, avoiding Evie's what-a-lousy-liar stare. Moaning ever so slightly, he rose from the table and walked slowly toward the men's room.

Orlando Bloom couldn't have done better, Andrew thought. When he was out of Pop's sight, he ran for the front door.

As Andrew stepped outside, the cool night swallowed

him. The mist, rolling up Franklin Street from the marina, shrouded the street in fog. He didn't have much time. In a few minutes, Pop would be wondering where he was.

He raced one block south to Franklin and Pacific and turned right, pulling the map out of his rear pocket. The check mark had been drawn very thinly, very precisely. But the map's scale was so small. It was impossible to tell exactly where he was supposed to look.

In the middle of the block was a vacant lot where a house had been torn down. It was fenced in and the ground was rubble — broken bricks and stones. On either side rose two four-story houses, one made of brick and the other stucco.

A police car cruised by slowly. Andrew whistled, strolling down the street and nodding to the cop as he passed.

When the car was gone, he ducked through a hole in the fence.

He walked closer to the brick house, his footsteps crunching on the debris. The fog cast everything in shades of gray, but as he drew closer he could see that one brick in the wall was different from the rest.

It seemed a little loose.

And it was painted blue.

Look for a blue brick, Mom's note had said. *Yank it out.*

He reached out and closed his fingers around the brick. He was able to shimmy it a bit, but it was in pretty tight, and his fingers were moist.

He wiped them on his pants and tried again. "Come on, baby . . ."

The brick moved a fraction of an inch, before his finger slipped away again.

He prepared to pull again.

SCCRRRRINK . . .

He jumped. It was the rusted fence. Someone was pulling it open.

Andrew turned, but could see nothing through the fog. But he could hear the pounding of footsteps.

Coming toward him.

Chapter Twelve

"*Andrew, that was the worst acting job I have ever seen!*"

The familiar voice cut through the fog like a siren. Andrew's tense body went slack. "You nearly gave me a heart attack! Evie? What are you doing here?"

"What is taking you so long?" Evie hissed.

Andrew gestured toward the blue brick. "If you hadn't interrupted me, I'd have pulled that out already."

"Four hands are better than two."

They both dug their fingers into the narrow gap around the brick and pulled. It came out in a sudden lurch, dropping to the rubble.

Andrew jumped aside and then looked inside the new rectangular hole. In the fog-diffused evening light, he almost didn't see the edge of a tightly folded sheet of paper. He pulled it out, and a small pile of dust and crushed brick spilled to the ground.

With Evie looking over his shoulder, Andrew held the paper so it caught the light of a streetlamp.

Bay Marina Herald-Patriot Newsletter
Red Takeover of Alcatraz?
by Jedson P. Flinders

SSDI

June 17, 1968 -- You read it here, folks.
This humble fisherman may not have the
education of those wishing to undermine
this country, but his eyes don't lie! On
many an occasion, whilst the rest of San
Francisco sleeps, I have seen the movement of vast quantities of material --
floating derricks carrying gigantic sea
serpents which, I have determined, are
enormous sections of roadbed. Tunnels!
Under cover of darkness and fog, they
are dropped into the sea. "You doddering
bay trawler, it's The Transbay Tube,"
you may say -- but no! This is happening
miles west, near Fisherman's Wharf, the
tubes pointing directly toward Alcatraz.
But Alcatraz is abandoned, you say. Then
why, I ask, in the rays of the rising
sun, have I spotted movement there? These
are not the ghosts of Al Capone and his
merry band.

To those who believe that the Communist menace is a thing of the past, to those who say that the vast network of tunnels under our own Chinatown is a mere legend and Alcatraz is home only to pelicans and flora, I pose this idea -- a neighborhood of Mao's men . . . a former island home to thieves and murderers . . . where else would be a friendlier welcome for the establishment of a Communist takeover of the United States?

On one early morn, when the fog was as thick as peat, I overheard, on a passing pleasure craft, talk of another system of tunnels, brand-new, to be built on the west side of our fair city, extending under the seat of the military in San Francisco, the Presidio itself! And I saw through my spyglass a blueprint, passed from hand to hand, a spidery arrangement, like a network of veins, all right angles and connections. In short, tunnels! To arms, men, against this imminent threat to our way of life!

"Whoa, this guy is a nut case," Evie said.

"But he's right about the tunnels," Andrew replied. "He just didn't realize they were being built by the U.S. government!"

"But all this stuff about the Presidio — that's miles away from Chinatown. It's over by the Golden Gate Bridge!"

"Well, the Presidio's a park now," Andrew said, "but it was a military base. That would seem like a logical place for the government to build a tunnel. But I don't get it. Mom sent us all the way here for *this?*"

A car engine purred loudly down the street, its headlights lancing the fog. Andrew and Evie watched it pass the lot, then suddenly back up.

The lights went out.

"A neighbor," Evie whispered.

"Let's get out of here," Andrew said.

Squeezing through the fence opening, they began to run, their footsteps echoing dully in the thick air. In the settling dusk, the street was almost dark.

From behind them, the car engine clanked softly into gear. Headlights blinked on.

"*Andrew, we're being followed!*" Evie whispered.

They turned onto Franklin, raced across the street, and ducked into Il Duomo. Breathless, they slinked past a long line of people waiting to get in. "Made it," Andrew said, looking over his shoulder into the darkness beyond the door.

"We look awful," Evie said. "Tuck in your shirt. Fix your hair. Look like you went to the bathroom to wash up. What's our alibi?"

"I was attacked by a little old man who was actually an alien —"

"No!" Evie thought quickly. "I heard your groans in the bathroom and had to go in to rescue you. Now *go*."

Andrew straightened himself out as best he could. He and Evie wended their way through the tables. Pop was still sitting there, his back to them. Three salads had been placed on the table.

As they slipped around him into their seats, Andrew said, "You'll never believe what happened in the bathroo —"

But he didn't finish his sentence. Pop's eyes were shut. His snores sawed softly across the table.

Evie's tense expression softened. "Wow, he really *was* tired."

"Should we wake him up?" Andrew asked.

"No. Let him think that we . . ." Evie's voice trailed off. Her eyes had darted toward the wide front window of the restaurant.

Andrew followed her glance. Across the street, an old Ford Thunderbird with rear fins and oversize whitewall tires had pulled to a stop. Only one of the car's black-tinted windows was open — the driver's.

Before it rolled shut, Andrew saw the unmistakable profile of Mrs. Franklin.

Chapter Thirteen

"*Hello, aloha, shalom, salaam, you've reached the Franklins. We're not home right now, so at the sound of the tone, please leave a message for Eulalia, Sedgewick, or Doreen.*"

"Still not there," Evie said.

As she turned off the cell and reached across the bed to put it on Andrew's desk, her brother's stomach gave a growl.

"Excuse you," she said. "Garlic?"

"No, tension. Lying to Pop wrecks my tummy."

Dinner had been tense. When Pop woke up, he wasn't his usual jolly self. Evie had wanted to talk about Mom, to follow up on the long conversation they'd had in the living room, but a public restaurant wasn't the right place for that. Pop seemed irritated and distracted, anyway. Which made three of them. Neither Andrew nor Evie could keep from looking at Mrs. Franklin's parked car during the whole meal.

Evie assumed Mrs. Franklin was the one who had tailed them down Pacific Avenue in her car. But why?

"Maybe you should IM Doreen," Evie suggested.

"To ask where her mother is?" Andrew said. "No way. She'll suspect something. Look, when the time is right, we'll find out. Mom's message warned us we're being tailed. She didn't say *who* would be tailing us. I thought she meant some enemy spy. We're lucky it's a friend. She's covering our backs."

"Something smells funny, Andrew. I mean, why tonight? She must have a *reason* for covering our backs. Something's up. Things are getting tighter. Maybe there's new trouble."

"Of course we're in trouble," Andrew said. "We know that already. Look, I think Mom just sent Mrs. Franklin as a backup. To make sure nothing went wrong. To make sure we got the message behind the blue brick."

She turned Jedson Flinders's article toward Andrew. "So what's the big deal about this? It's just an old article about the tunnels. We know about them already. And Mom *knows* we know. 'Running was smart' — she wrote that because she knew we'd been in the tunnel with Spy N and Spy O!"

Andrew scanned the note, tapping his fingers on his

desk. "This Flinders guy sounds totally wack. A conspiracy freak."

"He wrote this during the Cold War," Evie pointed out. "Lots of people thought the Communists were going to take over."

"What's SSDI? She wrote 'SSDI' across the top."

Evie shrugged. "It's probably a government document. Government docs always have stuff written on them. Probably some kind of classification code."

"I'll Google it." Andrew spun around to his computer, clattered away at the keyboard. As the results appeared, he leaned in and frowned. "Social Security Death Index. It's a search engine for dead people."

"She wrote the initial next to Jedson Flinders's name," Evie said.

Andrew clicked through to the SSDI link, which opened to a fill-in page. He typed the name JEDSON FLINDERS into the data boxes and pressed enter. In seconds the record appeared:

Name	Birth	Death	Age at Death	Last Residence
JEDSON FLINDERS	5 Jan 1914	18 June 1968	54	San Francisco, CA

"The eighteenth of June . . ." Andrew said.

"That's weird," Evie said. "The article came out June seventeenth. He died the next day."

"This doesn't say *how* he died," Andrew said, turning from the monitor. "Maybe it's not such a coincidence . . ."

Evie nodded. She knew exactly what Andrew was thinking.

Flinders was killed. For what he knew. All it took was a piece in a local newsletter, a rumor. Someone had stumbled on a Company secret and suffered the ultimate punishment.

That was why Mom wanted them to see the article.

"She's warning us," Evie said. "She's showing us how ruthless The Company is to people who find out stuff about them."

"Like Mom did . . ." Andrew gulped. "And we did . . ."

Suddenly Evie was glad that Mrs. Franklin had been tailing them. She hoped Mrs. Franklin was outside their house right now.

"We *are* in trouble," Evie said, spreading out the clues from Mom's box. "What does she want us to do? What do these clues mean — the fingerprinting kit, the map . . . ?"

"Evie, look what Flinders called the tunnels: '. . . *a spidery arrangement, like a network of veins, all right angles and connections.*'" Andrew held up the drawing on the clear sheet. "He could have been writing about *this*."

Evie looked closely. There had to be some further clue, some indication of how they were supposed to use this.

Her eye focused on the sheet's upper left-hand corner. It was strangely warped and curled. "Andrew, did you spill something on that?"

"No. Why?"

"This corner looks funny. Like it's been wet and then dried."

Andrew took the sheet and looked closely. "Or like someone wrote on it and then erased it."

"Invisible ink?" Evie said.

Andrew held it up against his lamplight. "It's not light-sensitive. Maybe you have to have, like, some special kind of pen . . ."

Pen. Evie reached into the pile of Mom's clues and picked up the felt-tip pen they had assumed was broken. "Maybe this is good for something after all."

Eagerly, Andrew took the pen and rubbed its tip over the paper's corner.

Slowly, a message appeared:

$$11\ 11\ 11 + 325$$
$$0010$$
$$37\ 47\ 27\ N$$
$$122\ 24\ 22\ W$$

SPY X

They both stared, flabbergasted and confused. "A number code and Mom's fingerprint," Evie said. "The print must have something to do with the kit."

"Let's start at the top," Andrew suggested. " 'Eleven

eleven eleven.' The day she left us, our eleventh birthday — 'plus three hundred twenty-five.' "

"That's got to mean three hundred twenty-five days," Evie said, grabbing a pencil and paper.

She worked backward. *Three hundred sixty-five days would be November eleventh . . . minus forty to make three-twenty-five . . . allowing for thirty-one days in October . . .* "Andrew, that's the day after tomorrow!"

"Really? What does that mean, Evie? What happens on that day? *What else does this note say?*"

Thump. Thump. Thump. Thump.

Pop's footsteps. Coming upstairs.

Andrew and Evie quickly shoved everything into Andrew's closet.

Pop knocked on the door and leaned into the room, his face haggard and grim. "Hi, guys. Just wanted to thank you for being good dinner partners. Sorry I was such a drip. Between my work schedule and Andrew's tummy . . . I think we all need our sleep tonight. So Evie, in your room, please. Lights out in five minutes, okay?"

"Okay, Pop," Evie said. "We just have a little bit more homework."

Pop nodded. "Okay, ten minutes."

As he left, Andrew raised an eyebrow. "It would be so

great if we could get his help," he whispered. "He'd be so good at this."

"Someday we won't have to keep secrets," Evie said with a wistful shrug. "Let's crack this thing and find Mom. She'll know how to handle Pop's suspicions."

Bleeeeep!

Evie was closer to the cell, so she grabbed it off the night table. "If it's another pizza order, I'm going to scream."

"That'll keep them from calling back," Andrew said.

But the phone's LCD screen said 1 TEXT MESSAGE.

Evie pressed ENTER and watched the words appear on the screen:

Get film.
Expose first.
Meet tomorrow
10:45 P.M.
SOS

"You were right," Andrew said, "something *is* up."

"Chatter . . ." Evie said under her breath. "That's what the FBI and CIA find right before some awful plot. Computer messages, notes, phone calls — they increase in number. Like now. Mom is really trying hard to reach us, Andrew. She's in big trouble."

"SOS," Andrew murmured. "This isn't even in code."

Evie began pacing. "What does she mean, 'Get film'? Do we even *have* film?"

"*Seven minutes!*" Pop bellowed from downstairs.

Andrew hopped off the bed and dug around in Mom's first box. "Remember this?" he said, pulling out a canister of film.

"Perfect! Now expose it, Andrew. That's what she wants us to do. Pull the film out and let the light hit it."

Andrew closed his fingers around the translucent brownish strip of film that stuck out of the canister. He pulled slowly. The film came out . . . one inch . . . two . . .

And suddenly, it wasn't film anymore, but a tough strip of thin plastic with a message printed on it:

HARRIET TUBMAN THOMAS PAINE://
192.168.265.7

"What the heck . . . ?" Andrew said.

"*Harriet Tubman . . . Thomas Paine . . .*" Evie murmured.

There had to be a connection. *Historical figures . . . courageous slave woman and brave Colonial writer . . .* They had bravery in common. What was it that Thomas Paine had done? He'd written something . . .

"*Common Sense!*" Evie exclaimed. "That's the name of the book Thomas Paine wrote, right? It must be a hint. Mom's telling us to use our common —"

"I did already," Andrew said, sitting at his computer.

"Did what?"

"Used my common sense. The colon and the two slashes gave it away." Andrew began typing at the keyboard. "Take the initials of Harriet Tubman Thomas Paine — HTTP. Those are the letters that appear before every web address. Hyper Text Transfer Protocol. Something like that. And those four numbers separated by dots? They look to me like an IP address."

"A who?"

"Every web address has a sequence of IP numbers," Andrew explained. "Four numerals. They're like coordinates that show the address's location in cyberspace."

He pointed to his browser's address bar, where he'd typed in http://192.168.265.7. When he pressed ENTER, a web page popped onto his screen.

A photo of the Golden Gate Bridge, with a zoom option.

An arrow pointed to a place near the base of the bridge. Andrew clicked on it, zooming in until he saw what was at the arrow's point.

He and Evie both leaned close to the screen, staring at the unlikely image.

"*This* is where we're supposed to meet Mom?" Andrew asked.

It was a manhole cover.

Chapter Fourteen

As usual, Andrew met his sister in the yard after school the next afternoon. It was Friday, and the air rang with gleeful screams.

"Are we set with the plan?" Evie asked as they headed out of the gate. "For tonight?"

"At ten-thirty *I'm* supposed to tell Pop I have to pick up poster board at the twenty-four/seven store, then I detour down to the bridge . . ."

"No, no, no — we rejected that plan!" Evie said. "Poster board on a Friday night? Pop's way too smart to fall for it. *You* were going to act sick, and *I* was going to run out at ten-thirty for an emergency bottle of ginger ale. Then *I* was going to find Mom at the manhole cover and call you on the cell."

Andrew gave her a look. "I don't understand why *you* get to do the cool part."

"*This is about more than coolness, Andrew Wall!*" Evie snapped. "It's the plan we agreed on. It makes the most sense. It's our best chance of finding Mom, and that's that."

"Fine," Andrew grumbled. "Just fine."

He would go along with Evie's idea. For the sake of peace and harmony.

But if it didn't work, he had an emergency plan of his own.

At precisely 10:25 that night, Evie raced downstairs. Pop was in the living room, reading the *Wall Street Journal*. "Gotta go," she said, pulling on a jacket. "Andrew's sick again. I'll pick up some ginger ale. Need anything?"

"Whoa . . . whoa . . . wait a minute," Pop said. "Don't we have some?"

Duh. She hadn't bothered to check. That was stupid. Really stupid.

"I don't think so," she said. "But we should have more, anyway. So I'll go, okay?"

"Do you see the time?" Pop asked. "Since when are you allowed out by yourself so late?"

"I'm almost *twelve*, Pop. And it's Friday night. It's totally safe. Everyone else goes out this late. The streets are crowded."

Pop reached for the living-room phone. "I'll call Ralph, over at the Pacifica Market. They deliver."

"*Wait!*" Evie screamed. "*Don't do that!*"

Pop cocked his head. "Evie, why are you so worked

up? It's just a stomach bug, right? Or do I need to take him to a doctor?"

"No! He's not that bad. It's just that . . . well, a phone delivery for one bottle of ginger ale? It's so expensive. The delivery charge will cost more than the bottle!"

"We can afford it." Pop began dialing the number. "Sorry, sweetie, but I can't let you outside at this hour. Especially with what's happened to your mom. This whole thing makes me very nervous. Who knows what's out there?"

"But — but —"

"Hi, Ralph?" Pop said into the phone. "Richard Wall here. Could you send over a liter bottle of ginger ale . . . ?"

Evie slunk back into the foyer, out of Pop's sight. Then she bolted up the stairs.

It was already 10:32. They would have to think of something fast.

Andrew's bedroom light was out. She flicked it on and saw her brother hunched under sheets and blankets, which he'd pulled over his head. "Get up, we have to think of something else," she said.

He didn't respond.

"Hey, lazybones!" She yanked the covers, and they slid off easily.

Too easily.

Andrew was gone. His pillows had been shaped to resemble a human body in fetal position.

A small yellow Post-it note lay on the bottom sheet: WILL CALL AT 10:45.

The sneak.

The double-crossing, glory-hogging sneak.

While she and Pop had been arguing, Andrew had managed to slip downstairs and out the back door.

He'd had his way after all.

Evie quickly pulled the covers back up over the pillows, arranging them as realistically as she could. Then she ran to the top of the stairs.

"*Pop?*" she called down. "*Andrew's feeling much better! You can cancel that ginger ale!*"

Approximately fifteen blocks away, at the corner of Marina and Baker, Andrew climbed out of a taxi. Hanging around his neck were two things his mom had sent in an earlier package — a powerful unidirectional microphone disguised as a cell phone, and a pair of collapsible binoculars.

He figured he'd need those. At night, especially in the fog, a spy had to extend his eyes and ears.

He was at the edge of the city, bounded by the bay to the north and the Pacific Ocean to the west. Along the bay, a path led through a narrow strip of park to the Golden Gate Bridge. This park was once a part of the old Army' base, this path a military road. Directly to the south, sitting darkly atop a steep hill, was the rest of the Presidio, acres and acres of forest, meadows, and abandoned brick barracks and houses.

As Andrew walked west, the fog billowed off the bay, and water lapped loudly against the pylons. A couple, giggling over a private joke, strolled past him in the opposite direction. A biker whizzed by. But they were the only ones who'd braved this uncomfortable night, and when they were gone, Andrew was alone. He began to shiver, the cold penetrating his bones.

Through the mists he could just barely see the lights of the enormous bridge. Tires whizzed along the roadbed that arched invisibly overhead.

Two-thirds of the way through the park, the base of the bridge came into view, a looming slab of concrete the size of an apartment building. As he neared it, he looked for the manhole cover.

There. About thirty feet from the base of the bridge. A black hole in the path.

It was open.

As he moved slowly closer, two figures emerged from the shadows beneath the bridge.

Andrew ducked behind a bush. The people were deep in conversation, a male and a female, both dressed in dark pants, sweatshirts, and knit caps. Their words were impossible to make out.

He wiped his fog-moistened hands on his jacket and inserted the mike's earphones, then held out the microphone itself toward the couple.

". . . if they don't come?" a male voice said softly.

"We got them once," a female voice replied. "We'll get them again — if not today, fine, we'll send them more clues. They love clues."

They love clues.

They were talking about Andrew and Evie. And he knew the voice. He knew it well.

To be sure, he took out the binocs and peered through. They were light-enhanced, and as the two stepped through a dim pool of streetlamp light, Andrew caught a glimpse of a face that seemed to make the temperature of the air drop another ten degrees.

Marisol.

Chapter Fifteen

Pacing in her bedroom, Evie looked at her clock. 10:53. *Will call at 10:45*, Andrew had written.

Yeah, right.

She knew what had happened. He'd met Mom already — *that's* what had happened.

Right now they were hugging and kissing. Skipping down the road in that nice little park by the bay. Strolling over to Ghirardelli Square for some ice cream.

Was Ghirardelli Square open at this hour?

It was so unfair.

She did all the heavy brainwork, and Andrew got his way. Now *she* had to stay home, pacing her room, listening to the sound of Pop's fingers clicking and clacking on his office computer keyboard downstairs.

Evie flopped onto her bed. She had laid the contents of Mom's second box over her bedspread, and they bounced, the fingerprint kit sliding to the floor. Some of the dust spilled onto the carpet, but that would be easy to clean.

As she picked up the kit, she glanced at the bedpost, where she had just isolated some of her own fingerprints. That had been fun, sort of.

Evie glanced at Mom's note:

11 11 11 + 325
0010
37 47 27 N
122 24 22 W

SPY X

Mom's print was nice. Simple and elegant. Evie hated her own fingerprint, which seemed all complicated and ugly by comparison. Funny how prints could be so different from person to person, if you knew how to look at them.

Halfheartedly, Evie dusted the note — and found a

few other prints. She looked at them with the kit's magnifying glass.

Yup. All the same. Mom must have done that on purpose, pressing the same finger down again and again. Her way of teaching Andrew and Evie how to identify fingerprints.

Always teaching.

Evie sighed. They had learned so much from Mom in the last few weeks. A crash course in spying. She had trained them well.

Someday, when Mom was finally out of hiding, Evie would make her continue the training. In person.

Part of her wanted to believe that that someday would be tonight, at the manhole cover near the Golden Gate Bridge. But her jealous dreams of Andrew and Mom and Ghirardelli were fading. They were just that — dreams. She knew better. Mom would no sooner be able to traipse through San Francisco than fly to Mars. People were after her. This meeting with Andrew was a good thing — it meant face-to-face contact at last — but it couldn't possibly mean Mom was free. She may have needed to pass something to Andrew and Evie in person. Or maybe Mom wouldn't even be there — she'd send a messenger. The risk of exposure would be too great — for Andrew and herself. The Company, after all, was on the warpath. They killed people they didn't like.

Killed them.

Evie glanced at her watch. It was edging closer to 11:00 now.

Where was Andrew?

She had to concentrate. To keep her mind focused. He was in Mom's care. She wouldn't have put him in danger. She wouldn't let him fall into the kind of trap they'd found at Alcatraz. Mom wasn't a person to be crossed twice.

Evie began pacing nervously. Andrew had promised to call. And if he'd really met Mom, she would have told him to call right away.

What if something had gone wrong?

She stared at Mom's coded note. Did it matter anymore what the note said? The cell phone SOS had come *afterward,* out of the blue. It had changed all plans. Most likely, the earlier message was now outdated.

Evie sat on the bed, idly running down the lines of the note.

Okay, "11 11 11 + 325" meant tomorrow. That much she and Andrew already knew.

The second line . . . "0010."

It was the way military people talked about time — "0010" would mean ten minutes after midnight.

Tomorrow . . . ten minutes after midnight . . .

If it was after midnight, then tomorrow was technically tonight — like, an hour from now.

The next two lines, "37 47 27 N" and "122 24 22 W." What on earth were they?

Locker combinations. Nah. No lock went up to 122.

IP addresses. Andrew had used that solution before. But IP addresses had four numbers. Andrew had made sure to pound that fact into her head. Each of these lines had only three numbers.

Besides, neither lockers nor Web addresses came with an N and a W.

North and *west?*

Evie scanned the map of San Francisco. It was divided by a lightly printed crosshatch of vertical and horizontal lines. On the map's borders, each line had a label. She read up the left side: "'37° 46' 30'' N . . . 37° 47' 00'' N . . . 37° 47' 30'' N . . .'"

And across the bottom: "'122° 23' 30'' W . . . 122° 24' 00'' W . . . 122° 24' 30'' W . . .'"

"Longitude and latitude," she murmured to herself.

She took the magnifying glass from the fingerprint

kit. Eyeing the longitude and latitude lines, she put a big dot in the place that matched Mom's coordinates:

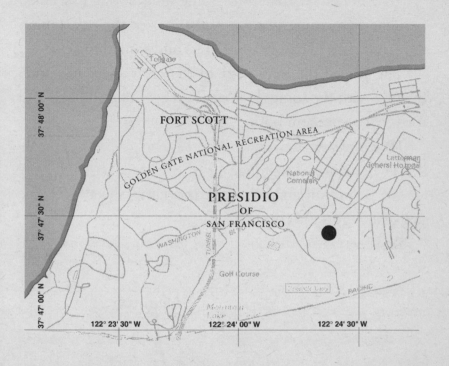

Odd.

"*Tonight,*" Evie said under her breath, "*ten minutes past midnight, in the middle of the Presidio . . .*"

What did it mean? Before the SOS came up, had Mom meant to send them on some kind of midnight scavenger hunt? Could that be it?

No way. Not at that hour. Not in a big, abandoned urban park.

Evie stared at that dot. Something about it seemed familiar. Something that reminded her of the *other* map, the street map of San Francisco — and something else . . .

She placed the map next to the clear sheet of paper, the one with the squiggly lines. Her eyes darted back and forth between them both.

And she saw it.

They belonged together.

Very carefully, she placed the clear sheet over the map, lining up the corners:

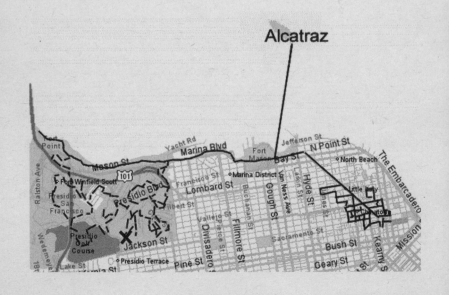

It was a perfect fit. The lines — the "spidery arrangement" — traced the contours of the city. On the right side, they ran along the streets of Chinatown. All solid lines there, connected to another solid line that ran to the Golden Gate Bridge. On the left, the lines were broken . . . like the lines of a road under construction . . .

Tunnels. They're all tunnels.

Evie's eyes settled on the X. It was directly over her dot — *the exact same place Mom had mapped out in her note.*

"What on earth . . . ?" she murmured.

Evie held the map close. The X seemed to be at the end of a tunnel. What did that mean? Did the tunnel open there?

She wanted us to meet her there. In the Presidio.

It made perfect sense. Why else would there be so much secrecy? And such a remote place?

But what about the cell phone message? What made Mom change her mind? Why the SOS — and why the meeting at the base of the bridge? It was a *more* exposed place, not less. It didn't really make sense.

The SOS was so clear. Right on the screen in black and white.

Black and white.

Evie stared at the pile of clues: the stuff from the first

box, which had led them to the mess hall and the trap in the tunnel; and the clues from the second box, the maps and the fingerprint kit.

She spread them out across the bedsheet. Both collections were full of twists and difficulties, both worthy of Mom. But looking at them side by side, she could see that the collections were different, too.

"Weird . . ." she murmured.

Everything in the most recent set of clues had Mom's handwriting all over it — the tunnel map, the fingerprint note, the "Mark Brick" message . . . even the note in Andrew's locker and the "SSDI" on the Flinders letter were obviously written by Mom.

But the stuff in the first box, the one that had led them into the tunnel, had been printed. The ripped note, the message in the film canister, even the e-mail with the "dumbwaiter" code — the cell phone message about the sink, too, come to think of it — all of it had been done electronically.

Was it a coincidence?

Evie rubbed her eyes. She was overthinking. It was important not to overthink. Mom had taught them that.

Better to focus on the fingerprint kit. On what *that* meant.

She studied Mom's print, memorizing its whorls and contours — just as she'd learned from the instruction book. Then she took out the fingerprint kit and carefully dusted the note from the film canister.

Andrew hadn't touched that message. He'd pulled the film from the end and held it out. The message had been at least two feet away from his outstretched hand. He'd held it like that as they read it. Any prints on the note would be Mom's.

Sure enough, the note was covered with prints. Evie ran the magnifying glass over each one.

Not one was a match to Mom's.

Evie dropped the glass. She ran to the closet and pulled out the empty box that had contained the first set of clues. She put it next to the second box — the one from the newspaper vending machine.

She dusted the surface of both boxes, inside and out.

It was nearly impossible to get good readings. She and Andrew had handled the boxes heavily. But there were at least seven of Mom's prints on the more recent box.

And none on the earlier one. The one from the car trunk.

"Oh my god . . ." Evie murmured.

The first box was a fake. Mom *hadn't* sent the night-vision glasses. Or the hints about the tunnel at Alcatraz. Or the film canister with the Web address. Or the text message at Alcatraz.

And if the first text message hadn't been from Mom, then neither was the second one, *the SOS about the meeting at the bridge* . . .

Evie checked her watch again. It was 11:11.

She felt the blood rushing from her face. She knew Andrew would not be calling tonight.

Chapter Sixteen

"Evie? What's up, sweetie?" Pop's voice called from his study.

"Tap-dancing," Evie replied, racing downstairs.

"Now? After eleven?"

"You don't know what it's like, Pop!" she shouted. "When you tap, your life changes. You get the urge when you least expect it. And, hey, it's Friday night . . ."

She was in the basement in seconds. She grabbed a CD off the rack — *The Susan Van Cott Tap Method, Advanced Beginners: Hear the Taps AND the Music!* — shoved it into the CD machine, and pressed PLAY, and then CONTINUOUS REPEAT.

As she raced to the key rack, an orchestra began playing *Swanee River*, to a loud accompaniment of taps:

Step-shuffle-STEP . . . step-shuffle-STEP . . . cramp roll, cramp roll . . . step-shuffle-STEP!

Ugh. The taps were *much* more professional-sounding than her own. Maybe Pop wouldn't notice.

She took the car keys and gently opened the door to the garage. Pop's GPS tracking device sat on a strip of Velcro on the dashboard. She ripped it off as quietly as she could and stuck it in her pocket. Then she ran back inside, up the stairs, and out the front door, taking care to close it softly.

The fog had thickened. The night had grown wintry cool. Evie could see her breath as she ran to the corner and turned right, down the long hill toward the bay. No taxis, right or left.

Her watch said 11:19. Andrew had been gone for over half an hour. She had to find him.

EEEEEEEE . . .

At Broadway a car nearly ran into her. A barrage of foul language told her she'd run against a red light.

Stay alive, just stay alive, she told herself.

The bay was coming closer. She could hear the slap of the water against the dock. She entered the park and ran toward the bridge blindly, the mist swirling around her face.

"Andrew!" she cried out. "*ANDREW!*"

In the shifting wisps of fog, Evie caught a glimpse of a distant silhouette. Maybe two. She couldn't tell.

She stopped short, out of breath. "Hello?" she managed to call out.

A bell buoy clanged in the bay.

Voices murmured in the distance. Two of them. She couldn't make out the words, but they sounded urgent.

Evie began running toward the sound.

But now she could hear other footsteps. Behind her. Coming fast.

She tried to spin around, but she was too late. A hand reached from behind her and closed around her mouth.

"*Mmmmppphhhh!*"

She drew her elbow upward, then shoved it back. Hard.

"*Ugh!*" Her assailant loosened the grip and fell back.

Evie sprang away. She ran toward the bridge, but footsteps from *that* direction were coming closer. "Who's there?" a voice cried out.

"Wait!" called another.

Spy O . . . and Marisol!

The bridge was not an option. She had to run.

Evie veered left — away from the bay. Toward a steep hill with exposed roots and rough sandy footholds. She clawed her way upward, tugging on the roots, digging her fingers into rocks. The ground slipped away beneath her, releasing small avalanches of dirt and sand.

At the top of the hill was a narrow footpath leading deep into a thick wood. Her feet caught on rocks and roots, but she moved fast, guided by the dull ambient light of the city. She was in the Presidio now. People had been known to get lost in the Presidio. She had to keep her wits about her. Head straight for the brightest illumination. Eventually, she'd come back out into the city.

Behind her, someone was running. Keeping pace. She veered right, off the path, her arms held out in front of her, beating back branches.

She nearly fell headfirst over a stout cement box. Some kind of small electrical switching station. Just big enough to hide a human being.

She dived behind it, listening for footsteps but hearing only the beating of her heart.

The crickets cheeped loudly. *Watch-it . . . watch-it . . .* they seemed to be saying. Overhead, a plane circled lazily toward the airport.

No footsteps, though.

She'd lost her assailants.

She needed a pay phone now. Andrew was in trouble. She looked to her right. The boxy shadows of the old abandoned army homes, lined up neatly like Monopoly houses, stood gray against the night.

She tried to figure out where the city was, but it was impossible in the thickness of this fog. She headed to her left, toward what seemed to be a road leading downhill.

The city had to be downhill. As she passed the last house, she was only vaguely aware of a movement in the shadows. Coming quickly, stealthily closer.

She leaped away and sprinted into the woods. But her foot caught on a root and she pitched forward, onto the soft grassy bed.

She felt a human body land on her, heavy and hard, knocking the scream from her lungs.

Chapter Seventeen

"What's with you, Evie?" a voice rang out. "Can't you ever stay still?"

Evie rolled away, out from under her brother. "*Andrew?*"

"You were supposed to be *home*," Andrew cried, getting back to his feet, his glare piercing the night. "I told you to be there. I told you I was going to call."

"You said ten-forty-five. I waited until after eleven!"

"*Pop* picked up the phone. I had to hang up!"

Evie stood, brushing herself off. "Andrew, you just *attacked* me!"

"You elbowed me in the stomach!"

"That was *you* down there in the Presidio?" Evie massaged her ribs where she'd fallen. "You attacked me *twice*? My own brother, *who I was coming to save?*"

"*I was trying to keep you from doing something stupid!*" Andrew took his sister by the arm and crouched behind a tree. "They were waiting for me, Evie. Marisol and Spy O. By the manhole cover. They were going to trap me. If it weren't for the fog, they'd have done it, too. They came looking, and I hid. I couldn't run. I was afraid they'd hear me or see me. I was hoping they'd disappear back into the tunnel, but they didn't. So I just waited. That's when I tried to call. With the phone on SILENT. I was taking a risk. But you didn't pick up!"

"I got worried," Evie said. "I came looking for you. Andrew, the note was a fraud. Mom didn't send it. She didn't send the first package at all — the one we found in the car. It was planted by someone else. Maybe Marisol. Or those two we saw in the tunnel."

"Wait . . . the infrared glasses, the cell block clue . . ."

"All a trap. The fingerprint kit proved it. The first box had none of Mom's prints on it. The second box was full of them. That's why we didn't find Mom under Alcatraz. She was never supposed to be there." Evie took Mom's most recent note out of her pocket. "But I cracked the code in the *real* message. The translation is this: at ten after midnight, we're supposed to go to thirty-seven degrees, forty-seven minutes, twenty-seven seconds North latitude, and one hundred twenty-two degrees, twenty-four minutes, twenty-two seconds West longitude!"

"That's a *translation?*"

"It's here in the Presidio — near the golf course." Evie showed him where she'd drawn the dot. Then she explained how she'd laid the tunnel diagram over the map — and how the X matched the location of her dot. "It's a tunnel opening, Andrew. I think this is for real. I think Mom is trying to meet us."

"Mom would *never* send us out of the house after midnight."

"Unless she were waiting for us." Evie looked at her watch, flicking on the bright greenish light. It was 12:06. "We have four minutes!" she said.

"Where are we supposed to go?" Andrew asked.

Evie took out the GPS device and glanced at its backlit screen:

37° 48' 09'' N

122° 23' 50'' W

"Are we close to that?" Andrew asked.

"I don't know!"

From the trees, a voice suddenly shouted, "*THERE THEY ARE!*"

A flashlight beam hit Evie square in the face. She stuck the GPS device in her pocket and took her brother's hand. Together they raced into the woods, blundering through the brambles. Behind them, footsteps sounded on the path. The flashlight's beam careened through the treetops.

Thump.

Andrew fell to the ground. "OW!" he shouted.

"Get up!" Evie whispered.

"Go! Just go!"

He scrambled to his feet and ran, following his sister into a clearing, and then a paved pathway under an elevated highway. The whizzing of the cars was loud, drowning out any other sound.

They were climbing. Evie could feel it in her thighs. She looked over her shoulder, out of breath. Andrew was urging her on.

They emerged in a wide graveyard. Tombstones rose out of the ground like a classroom of square-shouldered gnomes — rows and rows of them separated by curved paths. Evie stopped. Her heart was beating so hard, she thought it would break through her chest.

Andrew took the lead, across the cemetery and into another path leading into the woods. They crossed one paved path and then another, some with street signs — Arguello Boulevard — before plunging onto one more dirt path . . .

Finally, Evie's knees gave way. "I . . . can't . . ." she gasped, slumping against a tree. "I'm not . . . a long-distance runner . . ."

"Okay, you rest," Andrew said nervously, looking back through the woods. "I — I think we lost them. Can you figure out where we are?"

Evie pulled out the GPS device and glanced at the screen.

37° 47' 29'' N
122° 24' 19'' W

She unfolded Mom's note and held it in the device's LCD light.

37 47 27 N
122 24 22 W

"Andrew, look," Evie said. "We're almost exactly there! If we move along and watch how the numbers change . . ."

Andrew checked his watch. "It's fourteen minutes after twelve, Evie. We were supposed to meet her at twelve-ten. We're too late!"

Evie's heart sank. Mom was a military person. Twelve-ten meant twelve-ten. She hated lateness. When they were kids, she would leave the house without them if they weren't ready — and they'd have to catch up, tying their laces as they ran. *Someday you'll understand why promptness is important,* she always said. *Someday it could be life and death.*

Someday had arrived.

And they had blown it.

Evie stood. She fought back tears.

"Come on," Andrew insisted. "Get us where we need to go."

"She won't be there."

"We're *kids*. Mom knows we're not perfect."

Evie began to move. The GPS numbers changed. Slowly, they climbed a small hill. At the top was a clearing with a view over the Presidio. In the moving fog cover, a full moon struggled to assert itself, dappling the Pacific Ocean with a streak of amber.

"She's gone," Evie said softly. "We tried, Andrew. Let's go home before we're caught."

As she turned toward her brother, a figure appeared out of the mist. An old woman, walking a dog on a nearby road.

Evie stiffened. "Where'd she come from?" she whispered.

Andrew squinted into the distance. "Maybe we're closer to the streets than we think."

The woman was moving faster now, toward them. Her dog was yapping, trying to lunge toward them.

"*Let's get out of here!*" Andrew whispered.

The dog's teeth flashed in the darkness. Long, sharp teeth. Evie and Andrew spun around and bolted, racing back into the woods, downhill, away from Mom's coordinates, away from the slavering dog at their heels . . .

Out of the trees, two burly silhouettes appeared in their path. One on the left and one on the right. They shone flashlights into Andrew and Evie's faces.

Andrew flinched.

Evie took his arm and spun around.

The dog emerged from the shadows, growling, straining at the leash. Slowly, the strange woman moved toward them, into the light.

Evie's knees buckled. "It's . . . you."

Chapter Eighteen

"Stetson, will you *please* calm yourself!"

The leash tightened, and the dog pulled back, reluctantly quiet.

"Mrs. Digitalis?" Andrew squeaked. "*F-Foxglove?*"

Evie had to blink. It *was* her. The broad shoulders. The shoulder-length silver hair. The stern, deep-lined expression.

"So sorry this ungrateful cur scared you." Foxglove extended her right hand. "Rather a gloomy evening for a reacquaintance, don't you think? Although I've always felt you can smell the blossoms so much more vividly on a night like this."

As Evie numbly shook Foxglove's hand, a familiar deep voice behind her said, "Honeysuckle, I think. Isn't that right, dear?"

Evie turned to face the two silhouettes. The one with the flashlight swung the beam upward, catching both faces from below — Mr. and Mrs. Franklin. "Happy

Halloween!" they shouted in unison, breaking up into robust belly laughs.

Andrew slumped against a tree. "That is *so* not funny."

"How did you get here?" Evie asked Foxglove. "The last time we saw you, you were hopping a train!"

Foxglove sighed. "Ah yes, escaping a couple in black, as I recall. And now they're after you, aren't they?"

"And the last time we saw *you*," Andrew said to Mr. Franklin, "you were off looking for Mom with a tracking thingy."

"Onyx!" Evie corrected him. "Did you find her, Mr. Franklin? *Did you find Mom?*"

"I'm afraid I have to cut this delightful exchange short," Foxglove said abruptly, taking Mr. Franklin's flashlight and starting into the woods. "Follow me, please."

"Where?" Andrew demanded.

"In the fullness of time, all will be explained," Foxglove said.

Evie hurried behind her, followed by Andrew and then the Franklins.

They walked steadily downhill for a few yards before coming to a grassy area overlooking a small field.

"We'll keep a lookout," Mr. Franklin said. "Hurry, Foxglove."

An old cannon sat in the middle of the area, on a small concrete turret. Its barrel, cemented shut, pointed downhill. A pile of cannonballs had been stacked neatly in a pyramid nearby.

Foxglove flipped a hidden switch on the cannon. "Lift one of the cannonballs, please. And be quick about it. Both of you. One cannonball each."

Andrew and Evie did as they were told. The balls were solid metal and heavy.

"You will find two tree stumps along the edge of the grass," Foxglove continued, "each just large enough to fit one of those monstrous things."

"Found one!" Andrew called out, standing over a smooth round tree stump to the left of the cannon.

Evie spotted another directly in front of the cannon. As she trudged to it, Foxglove picked up one of the cannonballs as if it were a beach ball.

She stood over another stump, to the right of the - cannon.

"When I say 'Now,' place these dreadful things on the stumps," she said.

"I hear something!" Mrs. Franklin whispered. "They're coming!"

"Ready?" Foxglove said. "*Now!*"

Andrew and Evie did as they were told, lowering the metal ball onto the concave surface of the wood, where it rested snugly.

For a moment, nothing happened. Then the cannon began to move slowly to the right on a pivot at the edge of its turret, opening up a large hole in the ground.

"Bon voyage," Foxglove whispered, holding out her flashlight.

"We're supposed to go *down there?*" Andrew said.

Evie could hear a distant rustling in the woods. The shouts of urgent voices. "*Go!*" Mrs. Franklin urged. "They won't find you. They don't have the map of Minotaur II! But you do!"

"Minotaur II?" Andrew repeated.

"Just go before you get hurt," Foxglove said calmly. "You were taught to trust no one. But for the sake of your own lives, dears, you must trust *me*."

Hesitantly, Evie took the flashlight. "What's going to happen to you?"

"I," said Foxglove with a smile, "as always, will be fine."

Evie threw her arms around Foxglove's muscular shoulders, and kissed her good-bye. Then Evie shone the flashlight into the hole. A rope ladder descended downward, and she placed her foot on one of the rungs.

Andrew gave Foxglove a faint salute and followed his sister.

The old woman watched them for a moment, then disappeared over the edge of the hole. The cannon slid noisily back into place, plunging Andrew and Evie into darkness.

"Hey!" Andrew shouted.

Evie grabbed his ankle. "Come on."

They climbed down, slowly, carefully. The ladder shook. From above them came the sound of shouted voices.

Marisol. Spy O.

Were they alone? Had Foxglove and the Franklins escaped? It was impossible to tell.

Evie's feet touched bottom. "Made it," she said.

"We're going to die," Andrew replied nervously.

A cool breeze wafted around Evie, coming from her left. She swung the flashlight around. She was at the end of a tunnel, a cement wall to her right and a deep opening to her left. It seemed to angle slightly downward. She stepped tentatively into it, her feet splashing in a thin rivulet of water.

"Are there rats?" Andrew asked, his voice trembling.

"Just follow me," Evie replied.

The ceiling was low and they had to stoop. They walked down the incline, which grew steeper and steeper. Finally, Evie found herself clutching the walls, hoping she wouldn't slip and fall. She could hear Andrew's feet splashing noisily behind her. "Slow down!" she warned. "And be quiet."

"*Yeeeahhhhh!*"

He came sliding hard and fast. Too fast for Evie to duck out of the way.

She fell. They tumbled together, arms and legs ajumble, bumping over a slight ridge, pitching into the air, and then flying, belly down . . .

They landed with a loud *thwwurp* in a deep puddle of slime.

"Ohhhh, gross . . ." Evie said.

"I hope those weren't your best clothes," a voice echoed.

Evie shot to her feet. Moonlight filtered in through a grate high above, casting an eerie light into the underground chamber. The walls smelled of mildew, and the floor was coated with sticky mud, but Evie noticed none of that.

All that mattered was the face that seemed to float before her in the moonlight.

She found herself reaching out to touch the nose, the eyes, the lips, as if seeing and hearing weren't enough — as if touching were the only way to know that the face was not an illusion.

"Hello, dears . . ." said Mom.

Chapter Nineteen

"Woooo-HOOOOO!" Andrew whooped right in Evie's ear. On another day, she would have smacked him. Tonight it didn't matter. Tonight he could scream all he wanted.

Evie buried her face in Mom's neck, not letting her tears get in the way of the smell — the *Mom* smell, warm and earthy, a little like flowers and a lot like nothing else in the world. If she could have bottled it, she'd have kept it by her bedside this whole ten months and smelled it every day.

"Happy belated birthday, darlings," Mom said softly, in a voice that soothed and delighted, and Evie could no longer control her tears. "Have you been good to each other?"

"Evie was impossible," Andrew said, crying and giggling at the same time.

"Andrew was impossible," Evie replied at the same time — and just like that, she was laughing, laughing hysterically, and so were Andrew and Mom, their voices soaring and swirling upward into the cavernous room, until they both began shouting at once:

"Where have you been?"

"We missed you so much!"

"I thought I saw you at Fisherman's Wharf!"

"Who were those people — Spy N and Spy O?"

"Have you been in touch with Pop?"

Mom put her fingers to her lips. "*Sssshhhh*. We've tested this for soundproofing, but nothing's perfect. I know what happened to you. I know about Spy M and how she almost got hold of the Onyx device."

"Spy M — Marisol?" Evie asked.

"A code name," Mom replied. "I had no idea she'd been assigned to you. When Angel — Mr. Franklin — found me, he told me what happened. She'd found out about my messages. I figured it was a matter of time before her people sent you a decoy. A fake box. I was hoping to warn you first. But they're good — as you no doubt discovered."

"Marisol had keys to the house," Evie said slowly. "She was our nanny. She probably snuck into the basement and took Pop's car keys!"

"They're ruthless, too," Mom said, her face growing grim. "But I wasn't expecting they'd lure you into Minotaur."

"What were they going to do there — kill us?" Andrew asked.

"Goodness, no," Mom replied. "They were trying to flush me out. They figured if they kidnapped you, I'd find out — and I'd come get you. And they were right. I *would* have. But you were too smart for them. You managed to get away."

Evie looked her mother straight in the eye. "Mom, who are *they* — Marisol and Spy N and Spy O? Are they The Company?"

Mom's eyes dropped. "Yes."

"And you?" Andrew asked.

"I'm working against them," Mom replied.

Evie gave her brother a glance. His face was drawn tight.

"Why, Mom?" Evie asked.

Mom leaned against the wall. For a moment she was motionless, as if gathering a lifetime of thoughts.

"Once upon a time, I did work for The Company. It was a badge of honor — the elite top-secret international intelligence arm of the government during the Cold War. The code breakers' code breakers. No one — not one reporter — knew of our existence." Mom smiled, but her eyes were distant and sad. "I was recruited out of college, and I served proudly for years. Eventually, the management assigned their best planner, the woman you know as Foxglove, to teach me. I was on a track to which few people are invited — to the very top. She and I were a good team. Too good. We began discovering things. Crooked dealings, killings of innocent civilians —"

"Jedson Flinders . . ." Andrew said.

Mom nodded. "Yes. He was one of many who were . . . silenced. We found a secret file. An entire hit list of private U.S. citizens. Not only that — there was a squad of spies *within* The Company, trained to sniff out disloyalty. Any employee not toeing the line — or quitting — was made to . . . disappear. Forever."

Mom's voice trailed off.

"But you *did* quit," Evie said.

"Not at first," Mom said. "I tried to change it from within. But corruption is like rust. A tiny patch of it can grow to destroy the strongest metal. And when Foxglove decrypted a plan to take over the government — *our* government — we knew we had to act. We began picking up clues about a group of ex-Company employees called The Resistance. People like us, who had become disenchanted. All of their names were on The Company's hit list, of course."

"But these are The Company's tunnels, right?" Andrew said. "So how can *you* be here?"

Mom smiled. "The answer is in the box I sent you — the tunnel blueprint. Did you notice the paths of the broken lines?"

"Yes," Evie said. "They represent the tunnels under the Presidio! *These* tunnels."

"Minotaur II," Mom replied with a nod. "A modern *extension* of the tunnel system. The old tunnels — the ones written with solid lines — ran from Alcatraz to Chinatown, with a link to the Golden Gate Bridge. But The Company was expanding. It needed something more modern. Like anything else The Company did, the plans were kept secret. The paranoia was extreme back in the seventies. Not even the chief — the person we call Number One — knew the placement of the new tunnels. The only ones who knew were the Tunnel Supervisor and Crew."

"And that supervisor was — ?" Evie asked.

"Foxglove," Mom said, with a note of triumph in her voice. "And it will not surprise you to know that her entire crew was loyal to her. Every single one defected to The Resistance."

"Taking the secret plans with them," Andrew said.

"Precisely," Mom replied. "Minotaur II was never

completed, never connected to the original system. To this day, The Company has not found any openings."

"Have you been here all along?" Evie asked. "Since you left last year?"

Mom shook her head. "I got here, thanks to you. First you found Foxglove. That was important. I was hoping she'd contact me, but she was discovered and had to run. She did get news to me that a Mobile Resistance Unit had managed to hide an Onyx device in the Cable Car Museum. I had to get it to our permanent operatives here, the Franklins, so they could find me. And you managed to do that! The Franklins, by the way, had been part of Foxglove's team. They knew about the tunnels. I didn't. Even though she and I had been close, she'd never revealed their location — until Angel smuggled me here for safekeeping."

Andrew glanced around at the crudely built room. "So *this* is the headquarters of The Resistance?"

Mom laughed. "It's nicer — and bigger — farther in. Come. I'll take you there."

She began walking toward an opening in the far wall, training her own flashlight on the floor in front of them.

She was halfway there when the sound of distant echoing voices came from the hallway behind them.

Mom stiffened.

"Is that — ?" Andrew began.

"*Ssshh!*" Mom said, listening intently. "Follow me. Don't say a thing!"

Changing directions, she led Andrew and Evie to another opening, little more than a crevice in the wall. Inside, there was just enough crawl space for three.

Evie listened for the steps, which competed with the sound of her own heartbeat.

A beam of light swept into the room. Evie, Andrew, and Mom retreated as far into the crevice as they could.

"They're not here!" a voice announced.

Marisol.

Evie looked at her mother, trying to absorb the calm intensity of her face, trying to keep from thinking that everything Mom had hoped for was about to go up in smoke.

Another person moved into the room. Another flashlight. "They didn't just disappear."

A man's voice.

Andrew's throat closed up, emitting a tiny, strangled gasp.

Evie peeked out cautiously, following the swing of the two light beams, until one of them caught the newcomer's face.

"Keep going," he said. "Through that opening. Let's see where this baby leads."

And Evie watched, with utter disbelief, as Marisol ran into the next room.

Followed by Pop.

About the Author

Peter Lerangis is the author of *Smiler's Bones*, a historical novel; *Watchers*, an award-winning science-fiction/mystery series; *Antarctica*, a two-book exploration adventure; and *Abracadabra*, a hilarious series for younger readers. He has written several adaptations of hit movies, including *The Sixth Sense*. He is a Harvard graduate and lives in New York City with his wife, Tina deVaron, and their two sons, Nick and Joe.

We're looking for a few good kids.

ASA
AMERICAN **SPY** ACADEMY

DO YOU HAVE WHAT IT TAKES TO BE A SPY?

Find out at:
WWW.SCHOLASTIC.COM/SPYX

■ SCHOLASTIC

SPYXWT

Trust no one.

Keep away from strangers.

Say nothing.

Be extra careful.